"CAPTIVATING . . . ."
s. magazine

"QUICKLY PICKS UP SPEED AND TAKES THE READER ON AN EMOTIONAL AND VERY ENTERTAINING RIDE."
—*Richmond West County Times*

"A SNICKER-OUT-LOUD, THOUGHTFUL BOOK . . . CAUSTIC HUMOR SPIKES HER FLOWING PROSE."
—*Albuquerque Journal*

"UYEMOTO HAS A REAL LOVE OF WORDS. . . . THE PROTAGONIST SHE HAS CREATED IS THE PERFECT VEHICLE FOR HER YOUNG, CONFIDENT, AND WITTY VOICE."
—*Booklist*

"ENGAGING . . . SLY, CAUSTIC HUMOR . . . AN OFFBEAT MIX OF *THE BELL JAR* AND *THE JOY LUCK CLUB* THAT MAY APPEAL TO READERS OF EITHER."
—*Library Journal*

"ARTFULLY CRAFTED; IRONICALLY FUNNY BUT ALSO SERIOUS; CLEVER AND INSIGHTFUL. . . . UYEMOTO IS A WRITER WORTH WATCHING."
—*Pacific Reader*

"AN INSIGHTFUL, CATHARTIC NOVEL."
—*Publishers Weekly*

"WRITTEN WITH WRY HUMOR AND CLEAR LANGUAGE . . . A TRUTHFUL LOOK AT RELATIVES WHO MAY DRIVE US CRAZY BUT REMAIN, IN THE END, FAMILY."
—*Sacramento News & Review*

"TOUCHING, FUNNY AND TRUE."
—*Copley News Service*

HOLLY UYEMOTO, a fourth-generation Japanese American, left high school at the age of fifteen to become a novelist. She lives in Northern California and Albuquerque, New Mexico.

Holly Uyemoto

A PLUME BOOK

PLUME
Published by the Penguin Group
Penguin Books USA Inc., 375 Hudson Street, New York, New York 10014, U.S.A.
Penguin Books Ltd, 27 Wrights Lane, London W8 5TZ, England
Penguin Books Australia Ltd, Ringwood, Victoria, Australia
Penguin Books Canada Ltd, 10 Alcorn Avenue, Toronto, Ontario, Canada M4V 3B2
Penguin Books (N.Z.) Ltd, 182–190 Wairau Road, Auckland 10, New Zealand

Penguin Books Ltd, Registered Offices: Harmondsworth, Middlesex, England

Published by Plume, an imprint of Dutton Signet,
a division of Penguin Books USA Inc.
Previously published in a Dutton edition.

First Plume Printing, February, 1996
10 9 8 7 6 5 4 3 2 1

 REGISTERED TRADEMARK—MARCA REGISTRADA

The Library of Congress has catalogued the Dutton edition as follows:

Uyemoto, Holly.
Go / Holly Uyemoto.
p.   cm.
ISBN 0-525-93779-X (hc.)
ISBN 0-452-27197-5 (pbk.)
1. Young women—United States—Fiction.   2. Japanese American
families—Fiction.   3. Japanese American women—Fiction.
4. Japanese American—Fiction.   I. Title.
PS3571.Y68G6   1995
813'.54—dc20   94–31983
                                                          CIP

Printed in the United States of America
Original hardcover design by Steven N. Stathakis

PUBLISHER'S NOTE
This is a work of fiction. Names, characters, places, and incidents either are the product
of the author's imagination or are used fictitiously, and any resemblance to actual
persons, living or dead, events, or locales are entirely coincidental.

BOOKS ARE AVAILABLE AT QUANTITY DISCOUNTS WHEN USED TO PROMOTE PRODUCTS
OR SERVICES. FOR INFORMATION PLEASE WRITE TO PREMIUM MARKETING DIVISION,
PENGUIN BOOKS USA INC., 375 HUDSON STREET, NEW YORK, NY 10014.

For Eta Lin, WJF, and my dad

Ugly Duckling Boy

"**O**ne minute, there," he said. Ojiichan drew his cigarette across his throat in an eloquent gesture worthy of a theater star before an imperial audience. "Next, ha! Gone."

It was September of 1978. My parents and I were visiting my mother's parents' ranch in California. We did this every summer. In 1978, I turned six. Ojiichan was almost eighty, but he seemed ageless. We, his grandchildren, crowded around him on the veranda of the ranch house. He surveyed us from behind severe black glasses, the lenses of which magnified his stormy orbs.

In his presence, lungs constricted with fear, none of us drew breath. Ojiichan was telling of the turtles that terrorized his childhood village in Japan, ancient creatures who dragged their victims out to sea to be drowned and devoured.

Cigarette smoke curled around Ojiichan's hairy old lynx ears, reknowned within the Japanese-American community for the full lobes that could hold one uncooked grain of rice apiece. Everyone agreed that this meant good fortune. Ojiichan himself called that kind of thing "hoker poker" and put no faith in it. Luck held no place in his realm of interest.

He waggled his sparse brows at us, and beside me, my cousins Grace, Joy, Hope, and Faith sucked in a quick breath at the sight. The few eyebrow hairs Ojiichan had left were two inches long and swept his lashless lids. It was disconcerting to see his eyebrows and cigarette swivel toward us in accusatory unison.

"Where gone?" he asked us slyly, grinning, and the encircling smoke and twilight shadows made his stained teeth seem very large.

Though it was the thousandth time they had heard the story, my cousins, all girls and all older than me, screeched at decibels guaranteed to bring their mothers running out from the kitchen. My mother had cooked a birthday feast of my favorites: sashimi, peanut duck, sesame chicken salad, shrimp salad, teriyaki beef, caramel eggplant with pork, apricot chicken and carrots, and rice. Afterward, she and two of her sisters-in-law helped my grandmother with the dinner dishes. Together, they prepared the cake, ice cream, soda, and tea. Aunt May, excluded from after-dinner duty, drifted out from the dining room. The veranda was a fine place, set between the kitchen and the garden. From our positions around Ojiichan's great wicker throne, we could smell my mother's greatest creations—her cooking and her flowers—at the same time.

"You're scaring them," the three women, emerging from the kitchen, chastised their father-in-law. As he aged, his daughters-in-law addressed him with an ever-decreasing level of respect. He had weakened physically and mentally from the succession of strokes that eventually killed him before his ninetieth birthday. He was losing his sight. His daughters-in-law treated him like an old foreign thing who had somehow attached himself to the faux-leather recliner in front of the television when they weren't looking.

"*Sah*, look at them," brayed an aunt, speaking half in Japanese, half in English. "*Osoroshii, desu yo*! They frightened!" she accused Ojiichan.

"Not scared!" he insisted, and swept his dark hands, tough and brown after a lifetime of fishing and other labors, over us. "Never scared." He scorned his sons' wives, and his words were both a reprimand and a warning from the man who, throughout his life, had placed the highest premium imaginable on mental toughness and physical courage.

My cousins said nothing, huddled together, silent conspirators with their mothers. They knew well wherein their best interests lay and I thought them all contemptible, weak, and very female.

"I'm not scared," I announced fearlessly. "Tell about finding the fishermen's clothes later on."

Wily, more alert than he ever let on, Ojiichan's eyes slid to his daughters-in-law to gauge their reactions. His eyebrow hairs bobbed and fluttered in the breeze that brought us a whiff of chocolate from the kitchen and chlorine from the pool. Despite Ojiichan's resistance, my grandmother had insisted on the pool's installation, envisioning swimming parties for all the grandchildren she didn't yet have.

My aunts regarded both Ojiichan and me with distaste so palpable that had it been heat, we would have been incinerated. A double cremation; our teeth, mine tiny white tiles and Ojiichan's discolored from three packs a day but still all his own, would have been the only remaining evidence. They would clack and echo eternally in our respective urns.

"You have different upbringing from mine," the first aunt said, yanking my arm as a rebuke. Her name is Emiko, generally shortened to Em by everyone except my mother, who, with elaborate old country formality, calls her Emiko-san. Observing strict social convention, conversations with Aunt Em strain my mother's Americanized Japanese to exhaustion. Aunt Em came from Japan to marry my mother's eldest brother, Mas. Ojiichan arranged this with the best friend of Aunt Em's grandfather. Early on, Uncle Mas and Aunt Em had three miscarriages, four daughters, and a stillborn son. It was these among other disappointments great and small that strained their marriage like a used rubberband that had no pull, no give, no power to hold anything together.

The other setback to their relationship is that Uncle Mas doesn't speak. He can, he just doesn't. When pressed, he speaks in short sentences, never using two words when one would do. "Rice," he grunts. "Huh." "Yup." My grandmother once said he started running dry in a World War Two internment camp, and by the time he married, he was the Sphinx, his secrets all locked inside him. He never wanted to marry. He went on three chaperoned dates with Aunt Em before Ojiichan told him to show up in a suit at the Buddhist church at eleven in the morning the following Saturday. Uncle Mas's great dream had been to be a pilot, and then the Korean War came along—his opportunity—but Ojiichan forced him to marry and join the family business instead.

"You're different, Wil," Aunt Ann informed me. She didn't come from Japan, but her parents did, after World War One. She is a *Nisei*, second-generation American. She's married to my mother's second brother, Sen. Uncle Sen and his wife don't have anything positive to say on my mother's behalf, and my mother thinks that they've mismanaged their lives to the point of oxygen waste. So they're all about even in terms of mutual respect.

Aunt May echoed to me, "You're always different, Wil." This was farcical, and even Aunts Em and Ann, adversaries by nature and familial status, shared a look. Aunt May married my mother's third brother, Wes. This happened relatively late in the scheme of things. There were no bridesmaids at the Christmas wedding, but Uncle Mas and Aunt Em's daughters—Grace, Joy, Hope, and Faith—Uncle Sen and Aunt Ann's daughters—Ashley, Jennifer, and Katrina—and I all dressed identically in creamy velvet dresses and took part in the ceremony. Afterward, we threw rose petals at Uncle Wes and our new Aunt May. "For long-lasting happiness," we said, picking red and pink petals out of each other's hair only to throw them in the air again. At the reception, we passed out gold fans and cranes we had folded out of colorful paper. "So your good fortune will grow," we told the wedding guests, demonstrating with sweeping hands both the wings of the cranes unfolding and the fans unfurling with prosperity to come.

The fans and cranes failed. Uncle Wes and Aunt May were the first divorce in the family, although they still live together. They're each too stubborn to leave the house to the other, too poor to go into litigation. My mother says Uncle Wes has a sleeping pallet in the garage, with the dog.

In any event, I agreed with the aunts that I was different. I was certain I should have been a boy. I wanted a voice, feet, and height, all too vast for perfect Japanese-American girlishness, to correspond with my sex. Listening to Ojiichan recall his boyhood, I wished for the chance to have been one of the male villagers called upon to battle the turtles. It seemed a missed opportunity of grave consequence. I longed to be armed with a big stick and the occasion to pound on the scarred and eternal shells of my demons, physically vanquishing them, driving them back into the dark purple glory of the sea from which they came. If given the chance, I was certain I could prove my worth as a boy. Through desire and deed, I could become a boy carrying a big stick.

According to my cousins, I had already succeeded. They called me the Ugly Duckling Boy. They were the self-proclaimed Swan Girls. "But unlike the real ugly duckling," the Swan Girls told me haughtily, "you'll never grow up to be like us." At every family gathering, after cake and tea, they would enact their moniker in the darkened living room. Dusty records of flute and piano music were brought down off a high shelf, and the Swan Girls put on old recital tutus and bowed their heads at coy angles to scratchy Tchaikovsky. *Peter and the Wolf* still makes me think of little girls aglow, graceful and awkward as they turned and dipped and bumped into each other between the television and the sofa.

The sight made me laugh and laugh, to the annoyance of my aunts and mother. My laugh has prompted people unused to it and me to look around for the geese; the Swan Girls' laughs are delicate and confectionery, slightly pathological in my opinion, but nobody asks me. Though we're *Sansei*, third generation, small feet are still a virtue, ranked high with long hair and skin untouched by the light of day. My coloring is right, but I'm floating on boats. In the foyer my Buster Browns dwarfed the other pairs of shoes, as though the Jolly Green Giant had come for dinner.

My mother appeared in the doorway of the veranda, wiping her hands on a dishrag. "Are we ready to watch Mina blow out candles?" she asked. Sometimes she calls me "Wil," sometimes "Mina." "Everybody, go inside now, come on," my mother said, moving past my aunts to herd her obedient nieces into the house. "Coming, Papa?" she asked Ojiichan. When he didn't respond, she said loudly, "Come watch Mina blow out the candles, make her wish."

He gave his cigarette a final swivel and chew, then spat it out into the lawn without answering. Inside, after I had blown out the candles, my grandmother took him some cake and tea. He ground out his umpteenth cigarette in the frosting. "He gets more and more difficult," I heard my grandmother tell my mother in Japanese. "He's practically impossible."

Years later, after my grandmother was gone, Ojiichan's deterioration accelerated, confining him to his chair in the living room. We had moved to California by then, and my mother, Ojiichan's only living natural daughter, took on his care. As the wife of the eldest son, Aunt Em should have been the one to do this, but nobody wanted that. And Aunt May is so far outside the family, my mother resists her help with even menial kitchen chores. "You must sit down," my mother scolds whenever Aunt May so much as lifts a dishtowel. "Please don't trouble yourself." This deference could be construed as regard, but only the willfully unsuspecting would believe it to be true. Rather, in my mother's indirect way, my aunt's position as an outsider is forever underscored.

It was Aunt Ann who expressed her gratitude to my parents like this: "So generous!" she effused. "Thank you, thank you! Of course, you're lucky you don't have so much in your lives to give up." Aunt Ann is the kind of person whose compliments make the recipient feel worse than before she opens both sides of her mouth.

"You don't know what he's like," Aunt Ann said, warning my parents of Ojiichan. My father, the Mathematician, rolled his eyes at this and said nothing. He knew what Ojiichan was like, and he knew what the daughters-in-law were like. If Ojiichan's faculties hadn't seriously eroded by then, he would have thanked my parents for their care, too.

As relieved as they claimed themselves to be, alleviated of the burden of Ojiichan, the daughters-in-law still came skulking around. They picked apart my mother's caretaking skills, asked Ojiichan if he was regular in the basest of tones and terms, inspected his medications. The Swan Girls dropped by all the time. My parents and I had settled in at Ojiichan's ranch, what had been my grandmother's dream house, so they felt entitled to lurk until their mothers called them home for dinner. They dug through old photo albums and hovered like spiders, eating all our food.

Ojiichan, almost blind then, reached out from his chair as he was passed by. My aunts reprimanded him and slapped his hands away. My uncles, especially Uncle Mas, were uncomfortable in his diminished presence, he who had once so dominated their lives now doomed to groping for their comfort. The Swan Girls eluded his grasp, poked each other, and snickered amongst themselves.

In the end, the old man who had battled the sea turtles in Japan when he was a boy was nothing more than a dreaded sea turtle himself. He grappled for purchase on our persons with his claws, trying to haul us into his sea of memories, old man's speech, and impending death. One minute, he was there, and the next, ha! He was gone.

I used to sleep lightly and dream of the baleful glare of turtle eyes upon me, filled with an ancient red-rimmed fire that never condemned, merely accepted. I was both intimidated and thrilled by this gaze, wanting its acceptance as my own. I begged this of the turtle who visited me in the restless moments before lapsing into a fragile sleep fraught with dreams of choking, falling, my own death. My solitary bedtime dialogue was less calming than medication, too self-centered for prayer. Every night, I bruised my toes against the bed's baseboard, swimming to an unnamed shore in my sleep.

Now, I'm so heavily medicated, I sleep a solid eight hours a night, sometimes even ten. I wake to smooth, unsullied covers every morning, limbs arranged in the same positions as the night before. When I saw my ex-boyfriend at the grocery yesterday, he told me with some resentment that I look great. My friends say the same thing. If I do look good, it has a name: twelve-hundred milligrams of lithium daily. Applied internally and externally both, salt tightens a complexion beautifully.

For the first time in my life, I'm well rested. It's nice, but dull. It was such a departure, I hadn't known what to expect. When the ex and I were together, I was possessed by insomnia. Suffering laser beam eyes, my gaze seared holes in my dormitory walls while everybody else slept. I used to wake every morning to sheets ravaged by my angry grip. Hurrying to the dining commons for cereal and soft-serve before my morning classes, my legs ached like a dog's, a dog mad to run, chasing its dreams across milk-streaked night skies.

Yet ultimately, the turtle didn't speak, never blinked, and had no balm or wisdom for me. It occurs to me now that we probably didn't even speak the same language.

Wee, Wee, Wee

~~~~~~~~~~

I was in a hospital until recently—three weeks ago to be exact. It wasn't that different from the other institution in my life. I'll call the latter place Politically Correct University, or PCU, for short. The principal difference between the two is that I far preferred the hospital. I learned more, for one thing. And in the hospital, there were fewer drugs and fewer irritating people, and everybody wore wristbands instead of armbands.

Blue-banded people roamed the grounds at will. Yellows were locked inside the complex, but were allowed out with appropriate supervision. I was a yellow. Red meant restrictions to the point where dining in the commons with fellow lunatics was prohibited for fear the silverware would be smuggled out for unsanctioned purposes.

I never got the hang of how the band system worked. Bettina, a suicidal OCD (obsessive-compulsive disorder) Catholic, who thought there were Hare Krishnas and disenfranchised Russians plotting against her in Santa Barbara, was allowed the autonomy of a blue band while I starved for daylight. I could have told her that the Krishnas couldn't afford Santa Barbara and that the real dispossessed Commie hotbed is PCU, but there was no point in disturbing her further than she already was. Besides, I was just jealous of her comparative freedom. Not that she enjoyed it, spending her time outdoors poking through the bushes looking for men in orange sheets and whirling around when wind rattled the leaves, expecting to confront men bearing poisoned blinis ready to banjax her from behind.

I saw her from where I sat indoors, in art therapy, defining my inner soul as a tree. We were told to draw the tree, or, as was the case with Gloria and her multiple personalities, trees, that we felt best represented ourselves. We were instructed to draw them in the setting we perceived ourselves being in before arriving at the hospital.

"No, no, no, no, can't do that, no way, sorry, sorry, sorry, that's fine for Gloria, Hector, Vivian, Patricia, Wil, but not for me, me, me, me!" Lewis and his metronomic cadences went zooming out of the solarium, an attendant in hot pursuit. Except when tranquilized, Lewis hadn't stopped talking since he was brought in. He was fourteen, small for his age, the heir to a textile fortune now that his mother was dead and his older brother imprisoned:

Lewis had watched his brother stick their mother with a steak knife seventy-three times.

Like Bettina, Lewis was a blue-band. I didn't get it. I turned my attention to my tree. It was on a hill with a fence around it; the roots were proliferate and tough; the trunk was sturdy. The only other tree in the picture was an almost dead twig thing halfway out of the frame. It had two tired little leaves on it. That could have been my ex, my father (the Mathematician) and my mother, a collective tree. My periphery is crowded, my center full of me. I was surprised by how much my tree said about the way I felt. I hadn't been thinking anything in particular, drawing my tree. Maybe, What's next, potholders? But there it was, in ink on paper, my soul as defined by a subconscious landscaper.

Out the window, Lewis was darting over hill and dale, losing ground to his pursuer. The art therapist told me, "You can't overintellectualize a picture. Tell me what these marks on the trunk mean."

I shrugged, despising this woman's familiarity. "I have no idea," I muttered. My hand drifted to my throat as if to indulge in the tactile analogue to Lewis's manic chanting. My voicebox thrummed comfortingly. Beneath the art therapist's gaze, however, I quickly put my hand back in my lap, in the care of its mate. I have a pale, four-inch reminder of my childhood near-drowning in the ranch pool. Nobody can see it unless they get really close to me, but I'm always aware of it. Even when I can't see myself, I can feel that scar.

"What have you been 'scarred' by?"

The quotation marks punctuating her question turned me off even further. "Angst," I returned. I saw that Lewis was being hurried back to art therapy. I pushed myself back from the table, having drawn more than my fill. I was suddenly consumed with an unspecified longing, best described as the urge to grab the art therapist by the bangs and punch her in the face. I doubted that this was the outcome she desired, however, and strove for reason.

Thinking of my grandmother, I told the art therapist, "For a woman of my culture in another era, what you people diagnose in me as bi-polar disorder would have been dismissed as weakness of character. It would have been a sin."

"Sin, sin, sin, sin, sin, sin," chanted Lewis, who had been returned to the solarium, and now gripped a Crayola. His tree looked like a stick man with no head, a barren twig lacking ground to stand on. "Sin, sin, sin, sin!"

The art therapist ignored him, challenging me. "So what?" she asked.

"It's a waste of time. My grandmother never had the leisure to go crazy."

"You do," the art therapist said candidly. "What's wrong with that?"

I declined to elaborate.

"Like I said," she reiterated, turning her attention to someone else's tree, "you can't overintellectualize a picture."

I wasn't paying attention, pondering what other peoples' trees would look like. I imagined the ex's tree, a weedy fir consumed with decay, and for bad measure, on fire. My mother's tree would be glossy and leafy, but dying of slow thirst underneath bright greens. The Swan Girls' collective forest would look like Patricia's tree did.

Patricia's husband had just died. She had been married to him for thirty years. He had put her in the hospital five times. The survivor's pride that shone in her sunken eyes as she related this in group therapy was interesting and grotesque, like a bad car accident. I had thought what with the husband dead, Patricia would be sunning herself on a cruise, but she was a wreck. Bettina told me that Patricia's daughter brought Patricia in chewing on her grandson's catcher's mitt.

Patricia's tree was a fragile willow dominated by a big, thick oak in the center of the page. The oak was depicted in gothic swirls of texture and hue while the willow was hastily sketched in pencil, rootless and without color. No light shone on Patricia's mute trees, but that's what bigger trees do—block out light. Looking over her shoulder, chewing on my marker, I realized I could draw that kind of alienation. It's me blinking away moon particles after an eclipse, a long time in pitch darkness without air or sound or illumination.

In grammar school, white boys asked me if I knew kung fu. I've never taken a martial arts class, but when the ex and I split, I knew to change my perfume. It was basic self-defense. I went from Paris to Poison, and late that spring, the bees were fooled. I was not. I had hoped to banish the ghost of the ex by ridding myself of that which he loved, only to be plagued by swarms of stingers reminding me of my loss and change every time I stepped outside.

My mother smells like sun and the lemon verbena soap she uses. My cousin Faith smells expensive. Faith and my mother show up while I'm in the garden, harvesting late tomatoes. Professor Schrader has saved my life by lending me his house in exchange for garden care. He and his family have been on a two-month sabbatical, returning tomorrow. Today I go to the ranch until university resumes. My mother and Faith have come in separate cars, one for me, one for my things.

"Wil," Faith greets me.

"Faithless," I return. She and her sisters are Graceless, Joyless, Hopeless, and Faithless. My other cousins are Ashley and Jennifer, names that, in my estimation, are their own punishment.

With disdainful, pointed toes, Faith indicates a pile of greens dotted with rancid tomatoes. "What're these, mistakes?"

"Overplanted," I puff, straining to reach a rotting split. I throw it on the pile, Faith jumps back, and the flies circulate, then settle again.

"You just leave this stuff?"

I sit back and remove my gloves, wave them at the flies that swarm. "It's life's earliest lesson. Some things have to die in order for others to live." I glance at my mother, who's moving the hose, inspecting some squash, wrinkling her nose when a grasshopper alights on her skirt. Either despite or because I haven't seen her since the hospital three weeks ago, she avoids eye contact, wholly concerned with the vegetation that surrounds us.

"How does it look?" I ask the consummate gardener.

"That plant is almost dead," she says, flicking the hopper to the ground and mashing it with her shoe. She wipes her shoe on the grass.

I miss a beat. "But look how many are alive."

"Tough to kill a squash," my mother acknowledges. "Why don't you invite us in?"

They follow me into the house. Actually, my mother goes ahead. Faith drops down into a kitchen chair. "Where's the tea?" my mother asks.

"In the bag." I wash my hands. Food from a grocery expedition that took place yesterday isn't unloaded yet. The bags are on the counter. I was so freaked out when I came home, I set them down and went straight to bed.

" 'Red Zinger?' " My mother studies the box. "What is that? Hippie tea? This place is a mess."

Her tea ritual underway, my mother starts wiping the kitchen counters. Faith and I go to the front of the house and begin carting my boxes from the bedroom to the minivan. When I return to the bedroom, I see Faith has opened a box and is holding a dress up to her size 2 frame.

"This is so beautiful," she says, turning back and forth to admire her own reflection. It's a summer dress, pale silk beaded with a starburst of pearls that shimmers like lunar light. My grandmother made it for my mother when she was a bridesmaid in Aunt Ann's wedding, beading the pearls by hand. "I'm thinking about running for San Francisco cherry blossom queen next year," Faith announces.

"Good luck." I pick up a box of books. "That should be totally degrading."

"What jewelry do you wear with this? There's a big cash prize," Faith muses, still watching herself.

I stagger, navigating the doorway. "Like I said." Degrading! "Would you help me out here?"

She pushes the door open wider with her foot, and returns to her reflection. "Being queen was my boy-friend's idea."

"Gee," I puff, "why not marry the guy?"

She glows. "It's possible."

"Well, you're obviously Mike and Ike, you think alike." When she gives me a questioning look, I elaborate. "You both think you should be queen. You should trade in your car, hook up your boyfriend to a rickshaw. It wouldn't do for the queen's consort to get flabby."

She frowns. "He works out at Nautilus."

"Naw, the gym is for wimps. Hey, Ojiichan would say, 'Where else but America, you can win Her Royal Highness title?' " I maneuver the box outside. Faith fol-lows me, clutching the dress. "Are you helping me pack, or helping me unpack?" I ask her.

"Your mother said you've been in a bad mood," Faith lets me know. "You should wear this on your date next week." She folds the dress into even thirds and hands it to me. "Borrow Grandma's pearl clusters from your mother," she says authoritatively. "The ones Dad bought her in Hawaii."

"You must be on drugs." I toss the dress on top of the book box and slam the rear car door. "What are you nattering about now?"

"Your mother doesn't think you go out enough," Faith says, smirking. "She says you've been in a bad mood since you got dumped, so she asked me to set you up. His name is Jeff, he's third generation, too. I went to school with him, he graduated two years ago." Faith at-tends a good school over the mountains. The way UCLA is called University of Caucasians Lost in Asia, or USC is

University of Second Choice, PCU is known as a valet
school, because the only job available to its liberal arts
graduates is Parking Cars. "He wanted to take you out
for your birthday," she goes on, following me back up
the drive to the house, "but I explained about the ranch
tradition, the party you have every year. But if you like
him," she adds helpfully, "you could invite him over for
your birthday dinner. I've told him all about the ranch,
and I bet he'd love to stop by for a swim. Your mom has
the pool up and running."

"You're too much."

"What? Are you disappointed he's not white?"

"You and I don't worry about the same things."

"Well," she says dubiously, "I heard your last boyfriend was white. You know that's a bad idea. Remember
what happened to Hope." Her sister was disowned by
their parents for moving in with her boyfriend, Avery
Jones, bassist for Honky Inferno. Uncle Mas still hasn't
recovered.

I turn on the stairs and Faith almost bumps into me.
It takes me by surprise all over again how much my
mother and she resemble each other, as to some degree
all of the Swan Girls favor my mother just by being pretty
and tiny and sharing half of the same gene pool. "Not that
I'm going," I begin, "but does this guy Jeff expect me to
be like you?"

"Oh, come on." She lets out a little laugh, like jingle
bells. "I made sure to emphasize to him that you're much
more about *personality*."

I give her such a look, she takes a step back. "Well,
good," I say, and start up the stairs again. "I wouldn't
want to disappoint him."

Her tinkly laugh is nervous this time. "Sometimes I wonder about you, Wil," she says.

I should have grabbed her face and pushed her down the stairs. She who hesitates. "Sometimes I wonder about me, too," I say.

I don't remember exactly how long we were together for, except that as befits it, the relationship passed in gas. In the beginning, shy in each other's presence and hoping to please, we never farted in front of each other. This voluntary suppression was no mean feat considering we were both dying of scurvy at the time, bloated out to here with flatulence and teeth awiggle in their sockets after months of PCU dining commons fare. Later, the ex told me he went home from our early dates gaseous and sometimes totally nauseated from holding in the disastrous gastrointestinal results of Baked Bean Surprise. However, in trying to make a good impression on me, he willingly stifled any colonic outbursts that might have issued forth.

How romantic! He was mine. Soon, we were farting in each other's company as necessary, but never without a warning preceding and an apology thereafter. "Sorry, just wave that magazine around a little." This was the longest-lasting level of conduct between us, encompassing both the pre- and post-sexual periods of our relationship. It also included discussing how much time to spend with friends and with each other, whether or not I should take X (in the end he decided No, he didn't think he could stand to see me grinding my teeth and sweating), and other matters similar in nature that are best left to resolve themselves spontaneously in any relationship.

Hindsight is twenty-twenty. The next stage was aggressive farting, wherein I wrote a limerick entitled, ''Ballad to My Bed Warmer.'' This was when the ex and I would be drifting off to sleep or just waking up, he would hold me tight, and tepid warmth would bloom under the covers. Peoples' own farts don't bother them; I could fart in my bed, but it bugged me to have someone else farting in my bed.

It didn't bug me a lot, though. I came to be convinced that this was a manifestation of selflessness, an indicator of deep feeling. I believed that in my acceptance, I could prove myself and my love to a man who doubted me in the most impersonal way: He had been conditioned from birth to doubt everybody.

Because it wasn't enough, it wasn't to be. Soon, we were complaining bitterly about each other's lax nutritional habits, and pushing each other toward the fan after Burrito Nite. At our lowest point, we would be alone and would flare our nostrils in defense and accuse the other of having farted. In the course of our time together, we zoomed from strangers to lovers to enemies, our lower intestines and olfactory glands the chief barometers of our decline.

We've been apart over three months, which is clearly not long enough. Not including the grocery debacle yesterday, we've spoken once since the fat lady sang. It was a conversation that started out tentatively because I was in the hospital, but then escalated sonically. I called him in a vulnerable moment, between my stunted trees and fantasy potholders.

He was stricken to hear that I was hospitalized. ''Just don't tell anyone,'' I said.

"Trust me," he breathed. "Are you okay otherwise?"

"Fine."

"Really?" He sounded wary, as if navigating the possibility that I might be playing a trick on him.

"I swear. Look, I need to apologize."

"Jesus, Wil."

"Listen to me," I said slowly, "I'm like the woman in the commercial, washing my dirty dishes in lemon liquid: I can see clearly now, and I'm so, so sorry." He was silent. I fumbled on. This was the unfortunate hallmark of most of our dialogue: I never knew what to say to him. I hoped he would forgive me for the bi-polar stuff I was unaware of at the time, and for the things from the past I was scared to do anything about even as all that ugly history made me lonely and alone. But all my inner eloquence came to was a stammer and a mumble.

"Cut it out! Jesus! I accept your apology!" He was shouting. Coming from a bilingual family wherein each word and gesture is an existential current in a dry waterway, I'm no ubercommunicatrix, but shouting was this guy's preferred means of conversation.

There's no reason he shouldn't be dating. Yet at the grocery, I nearly sent the whole six-pack configuration tumbling down, vibrating with rage and sorrow that his taste has veered to hooved mammals. PCU is a place of microcosmic social dimension, and I knew the mutant-morph on his arm. The ex had always made fun of her, and now he's with her. Somehow, I feel left out.

She seems to be well below his sightline of judgmentalism. It was crucial to the ex that I was beautiful, intelligent, superior. I was never permitted to act silly or look like hell. Being an ugly idiot isn't my major at PCU, but my pedestal was tiny and nosebleed high. I had no room on it to be myself.

This limitation wrecked every aspect of our relationship, eventually, even the sexual. From the way we caught fire when we first met in a seminar, I thought it would be the last thing to go, but it was the first. He didn't like to see my head "down there," he didn't want my face in a pillow except for sleep, he didn't want me to be "degraded" in any way. The problem was, he viewed virtually everything as being degrading. "All sex is rape," the radical feminists on campus said, and it was as though the ex was living in deference to the cry. "You can degrade me a little bit," I joked, but he was adamant, and that meant brakes on the fun.

I never felt so undesirable as when I was with him: the more he loved me, the more he hated me, too. Toward the end, I had to fight to breathe deep. He touched my elbows, flanks, and hips delicately as if I were made of air and glass instead of flesh and bone. I struggled to be sure I was still there, still me. My friend called him The Procrastinator, because our conversations during sex usually went this way: "What about me?"

"I'll get to you later."

And later, "What about me?"

"I'll get to you next time."

When I did enjoy myself, the ex treated my pleasure as an affront. He told me one night that I looked funny having orgasms on top of him. Then he was mad when I was hurt: You know what your problem is, you have no sense of humor.

But our problems really began after he announced

that he loved me. I was the last to know; like everything else, he ran it by his friends first. "He thinks he loves you," the ex's best friend told me one day right after Christmas while we walked back to the dorms. The ex was so out of touch with his feelings he had to run his emotions by consensus. His love wasn't an act or choice of feeling and generosity but a decree as spontaneous as a NASA launch.

The stone was cast, a death sentence. It was bad luck that I got pregnant. Pregnancy, abortion, breakdown. What's next, locusts? Condoms aren't foolproof: Some fool always comes along. When we met, the ex nattered on and on about hedonism as though he had engineered its invention. As though it were a toss up. The OED was going to call it Jakeism, but went with Billy Joe Bob Pierre Hedon instead.

But I cured his flapjawing. I turned the man impotent. Presently, I'm considering possible employment as rental birth control for citizens of Third World countries. Juan and Maria apply, I fly the friendly skies, and Juan's equipment shrivels to nothing from my mere propinquity. Ojiichan used to say all the time that you can't go through life without a skill. This could be my chance. Besides, for the cost of airfare and all the beans, tortillas, and horchata I can consume, I'm a damn bargain.

I never mentioned the abortion to the ex because the occasion never arose. Even the practicalities seemed too vast to be overcome. Would I have called? Written a letter? Dropped by? Stood on his doorstep and wept? Assuming I could have rented an asbestos suit and gotten past his hostility somehow, would he have given me "his half" of the money instead of getting a new motorcycle helmet or going to the Pixies' concert in both San Jose and San Francisco? Not that I was foremost concerned about money. Sensitivity would have sufficed. But this was the man who sneered that I should have played hard-to-get, who seemed disgusted that I had great orgasms, and who told me in his bizarre way—suspicious and downtrodden both—that it wasn't him personally, I could probably respond to anyone. I had thought I was the late-blooming type. Yet he was accusing me of indiscriminate response. We never communicated very well.

By then, we were in counseling together, at first trying to save the relationship but ultimately settling for saving ourselves. Therapy was First World torture. I finally told the ex that our problem was we never got beyond congratulating ourselves for being in therapy to take advantage of it. The concept was more appealing than the reality, accurately reflecting the relationship itself.

And here I am, months after the fact, crying, wee, wee, wee, all the way home. My mother and Faith scrub down the floors, sanitize both bathrooms, even tidy the garden with a rake and hose. My mother inspects her handiwork, circling the kitchen slowly. For years after the war, she and her family ate every meal in two shifts. They were so poor, there were only three plates, one fork, one pair of chopsticks, and a spoon. Ojiichan, Uncles Sen and Wes ate together, then my grandmother, Uncle Mas, and my mother.

My mother disapproves of Nancy Schrader's kitchen. My mother has five sets of china, eight to twelve place settings each, and at least five sets of silver. Her teacup collection is both functional and historically significant. My cousin Joy is trying to get her to change her mind, but I know my mother willed the collection to a museum, rightly thinking that I wouldn't appreciate it the way someone who cares would.

On the other hand, Nancy Schrader made her own plates, bowls, and goblets on a potter's wheel, then fired them in her backyard kiln. There's one for each member of the family, their names written on their respective place settings in glaze, abstract and wild.

"We have to clean," my mother says, scrubbing at the stained grouting of the kitchen tile. She looks like an ad for Lady Macbeth Spot Removal. "Get me a sponge."

"They're kind of hippies," I explain to my mother, meaning the Schraders. "Trust me, they won't care." When she looks incredulous, I add, "You're the only one who cares."

My mother draws herself up to her full height of four feet, eleven inches. She used to claim she was five feet tall, but her vertebrae have begun to compress, and now she's actually about four feet ten. "Allow her her fiction," The Math sometimes grumbles, and I do.

"It was an imposition for you to stay here when you could have come home," she says. "Why didn't you come home? I don't understand. But I can make it like you were never here at all," she promises me, and her glance is both reproachful and enragingly kind until she sees the look on my face. She frowns, puzzled. "What?"

Belly Language

~~~~~~~~~~

In 1941, all people of Japanese descent in America were classified as Enemy Aliens. Japanese cultural effects and anything deemed potentially useful in espionage situations were declared contraband. Before they went into internment camp, the Japanese-Americans' razors, knives, artwork, Buddhist and Shinto shrines, and photographic equipment were confiscated by the government. Hence, there were no baby pictures of my mother, born in a camp, and throughout her youth, her brothers—Mas, Sen, and Wes—told my mother that she had been adopted. There were no pictures of her until she was almost four years old.

When she was born, America had just declared war

on Japan, and Ojiichan was taken away for questioning by the FBI. In a heavily censored letter that arrived without a return address or postmark, Ojiichan instructed Uncle Mas to give my mother a good American name. He complied, calling her Ava after Ava Gardner. When she was a girl, she complained, "Why couldn't I have been named something normal, like Joan for Joan Crawford, or Carole, after Carole Lombard?"

"You're lucky you're not Lulu," Uncle Wes would say, "for, 'Little Lulu.' "

"Or Wes," my mother would taunt him, "for Western." Uncle Wes, born two years before my mother, was also named by Uncle Mas, whose teenaged cinematic preferences had ranged from southern vixens to cowboys running varmints out of town.

When they returned to California, Ojiichan took in boarders at the house he had convinced a Chinese family to rent to him. The house sat on an abandoned acre once belonging to a Japanese farming couple. The land had been left in care of former friends of the couple, but the friends didn't think the Japanese would ever come back, so they sold the property to a Chinese family. The Chinese family reparceled the land into plots and leased the plots out to tenant farmers.

As they always did, Ojiichan's ideas deviated from the norm. On his rental property, there was a small two-story house, a garden that had gone to seed, a ramshackle outhouse in which black widows and milk snakes lived, and a rusty old chicken coop. At Ojiichan's direction, the whole family crammed into the chicken coop, a humbler structure than even the sixteen-by-forty barrack they had all lived in in camp.

A plywood wall separated the humans from the chickens, who hadn't gone anywhere on account of the new human tenants: The chickens lived there, too. In Japan, my grandmother and her sister had kept a rooster as a pet. He crowed when the sun rose, chasing away the evil night spirits. Now, my grandmother cohabitated with the chickens whose status, in Ojiichan's poverty, had been elevated to that of family members.

Feathers were in the bedcovers, the rice, in everybody's hair. The rooster alighted on the hens and pulled great tufts from their backs and wings struggling to stay aboard long enough to fertilize an egg or two. The hens slept with the boys in the winter, everybody keeping one another warm. Their eggs were collected by my grandmother. Their droppings were scrupulously scooped up and saved in red Hills Brothers coffee cans that my grandmother brought back to the coop from her job as a domestic. In turn, the chickens and cans gave my mother the only job she's ever held: flipping chicken shit over with a paint scraper so that it dried in the sun for garden fertilizer.

Meanwhile, the house on the plot was wall-to-wall cots and straw mattresses upstairs and down, occupied by Japanese men who had preceded their families home from camp trying to find work, resting and refueling at what Ojiichan had named the Esperanza Hotel.

"You used to speak Spanish?" I asked disbelievingly. By the time I came along, Ojiichan had barely retained some of the once-flawless English and could only get by in his native Japanese.

"I know some word," Ojiichan replied arrogantly. "Learn fast, no matter what language. Don't so surprise!"

He knew *si, gracias*, and *mañana*. He knew *esperanza*, hope,
and liked its ring.

My grandmother was in charge of the children, laundry, and the garden. Under instruction from Ojiichan to
grow enough food to feed the boarders as well as the
family, she devoted most of her time to the garden. Ojiichan was in direct competition for boarders with the Buddhist church, which had set up a dormitory in the rectory.
However, the Buddhists couldn't afford to serve meals and
didn't allow gambling. Ojiichan had go, poker, and a garden. He met every train that stopped in nearby Sacramento
until the small house was bursting with recently returned
Japanese, the new itinerant labor force.

It was during this time, growing food, laundering
linens and clothes, and cleaning up after thirty to fifty
people, that my grandmother began to dream of a large
house, separate bedrooms, new, unoccupied white wicker
furniture on a cool porch. She admired the breezy flow-
erbeds she saw on the white side of town, where she
worked. All that lush color made her long for color of her
own. Tomatoes and eggplants aside, her garden had to be
wholly green. Any deviation, the yellow of overwatering
or the greenish-white of nitrogen deficiency, would have
incurred Ojiichan's wrath. Ojiichan had a low threshold
of tolerance for mistakes. So long as she ran it produc-
tively, in the garden my grandmother was left alone.

By all accounts, my grandmother never grew and
seldom ate another vegetable after the boarding house shut
down in late 1949, though later, she wasn't adverse to
nasturtiums or pansies in soups or on the tops of cakes for
special occasions. As with all things, memory is selective.
My mother says that as far back as she can recall, the only

time her mother had any peace was in the garden. Her brothers barely remember the garden at all.

"That plot a weeds, fer Chrissake?" Uncle Wes once asked my mother. "I thought Mama went there to get away from Pop and all his crazy ideas."

"Those weeds fed you," my mother said.

My uncles don't remember telling my mother she was adopted, either. "No baby pictures of you because camera got taken," Uncle Sen said, chuffing his cigarette. "Armed with Minoltas, see, we mighta helped the Japanese win the war."

Sunk deep in his chair, Uncle Mas snorted at this, and shook his head.

"Takes airpower to win war," Uncle Sen translated for his older brother. "Masa would know."

Uncle Mas could have flown a plane in the Korean War, but Ojiichan made sure he got married and had a child instead. My mother says Ojiichan liked Grace as much as he could like any female grandchild. Uncle Mas's firstborn, her arrival ensured her father's duty to Ojiichan. Uncle Mas desired the opportunity to learn to fly, but kept earthbound by his father's dreams, he settled down and began raising a family instead.

Before he bought a home for himself and my grandmother, Ojiichan insisted Uncle Mas and Aunt Em move into a five-bedroom two-story house in a good neighborhood. Ojiichan provided the down payment. At the housewarming party, my grandmother went and cried in one of the three baths. Uncle Sen spilled his drink on the living room carpet, causing a permanent stain despite all of the womens' efforts with club soda and Bon Ami. Ojiichan brushed off Aunt Em's formal, effusive thanks. "Fill bedrooms,'' was his only response, and though the bedrooms gradually filled, it was not with sons.

As Uncle Mas's daughters went away to college or got married or disowned, the house emptied again. Everyone has lives of their own now, leaving Uncle Mas and Aunt Em to rattle around alone on their dark threshold. Grace works in the city. Joy is married, with a young son and a new baby boy. Faith is working on her Mrs. degree. Hope was disowned for premarital cohabitation. Aunt Em's immediate response was insisting that Hope return her black BMW, license plate HOPEJET, leaving it in front of the house with the keys under the seat. Aunt Em couldn't understand how Hope could do this to her parents. What was she, Em, supposed to tell the family and their friends? Hope said she would never be able to become herself with her parents. She wanted to be free to live her own life, not the life her parents chose for her. Uncle Mas was clearly enraged, although all he could seem to articulate was that he himself had been a virgin until he was thirty. My mother tells me again and again of Uncle Mas's badge of virtue, bringing it up in an array of contexts.

The last time I saw the whole family, except for Hope, was at Uncle Sen's house earlier this summer. Uncle Sen and Aunt Ann have two daughters, Ashley and Jennifer. Their third daughter, Katrina Elisabeth, died in an accident. She was Kiki until the accident, whereupon she became Katrina. The first time Uncle Sen redid the house was six months after Katrina died. From after her death many years ago right up until the present, renovation became a bi-annual undertaking at Uncle Sen and Aunt Ann's house. At the beginning of this summer, Uncle Sen

and his wife were having a party celebrating the comple-
tion of their latest frenzy of home improvement. My uncles were clustered around Uncle Sen's custom-designed
entertainment center, letting Uncle Sen demonstrate how
his new bar swiveled out from what looked like regular
book shelves.

With the men in the family leaning over the bar like
that, I saw that the backs of their heads were flat. Americans put babies on their stomachs, but Japanese put them
on their backs. Raised in America as Japanese by my grandmother, all three uncles, at various stages of hair loss, have
plateaux where there should be cradle of bone and brain.
This may be what enables them to think in their flat, linear
way, suppressing all impulses toward madness and magic,
good and bad. If any one of them were lying on their faces
on a couch, I could eat M&Ms off the backs of their heads.

The fake book shelves were actually full of rocks, the
ones Ojiichan had collected and for which he had made
polished wood bases. Except for rocks, Ojiichan had no
hobbies, probably because he never had any spare time. In
camp, with no job and nothing to do, he developed an
interest in minerals and a talent for shaping wood pedestals
that illuminated the rocks' natural beauty. Uncle Sen took
most of Ojiichan's rocks from the ranch when Ojiichan
died. On his new shelves, Uncle Sen had a collection of
leather-bound classics with uncracked bindings, atlases,
three encyclopedia sets, but mostly, he had rocks. "That's
Sen," my mother said later, "full of more rocks than
books."

At the party my mother was swanlike in her mute
grace, gliding here and there with drinks and equally
sparkly small talk. During the cocktail hour, my mother

and Aunt Ann helped Uncle Sen, bartender on the loose, with the drinks. Then they, my aunts, cousins, and assorted friends adjourned to the front drawing room to admire Aunt Ann's *kokeshi* doll collection and each other's outfits and haircuts. Huddled together in tight knots of twos and threes, they talked about anybody who wasn't there to defend themselves.

I heard my mother say that the end of school had been tough on me this year. I didn't look their way, but she was glaring at me like I was the demon seed, her little Frankenstein. The disturbing vocal pitches of the women in my family put me in mind of malarial mosquitoes as they twittered madly. In the corner, Uncle Sen's two golden retrievers, Coaster and Blue, put their paws over their own ears.

Depression pierced every sheaf and layer of my consciousness—and my conscience. I viewed them all as though held in the sway of an out-of-mind experience. School had let out for the summer earlier that month, and I was at my hollow-eyed, post-abortion worst, sitting alone with a plate of untouched food on my knee, most of it inedible to me, all of it of the protein variety. My mother and her brothers have a deep-seated loathing of vegetables and a shared compulsion to put meat in even the occasional salad. Uncle Mas is the only one who doesn't eat meat, only because he can't. He has a weak stomach. Still, to my mother and her brothers, the only thing worse and more inexplicable than being stupid, lazy, or a Democrat is being a vegetarian.

Being a history major doesn't merit wild hurrahs, either. At one point, my aunts and cousins converged upon my dark corner, asking about my academic career and marriage prospects, both dim at best.

"What kind of history do you study?" one of my mother's friends asked me.

"American," I mumbled, and cleared my throat. "World War Two," I elaborated. "The internment."

"The internment," she repeated tentatively, certain my pronouncement was a cruel hoax and I would soon relieve her anxiety by hitting her shoulder and saying, "No, actually, I'm pre-med."

"Do you like it?" I was asked.

For all involved, there's nothing quite so socially imprisoning as politeness. Before I could formulate a worthy rejoinder, my mother interrupted.

"Wil loves to study other peoples' mistakes," she said. Head lifted in her characteristic gesture of pride and defense, she turned to me. "Isn't that all history is, dwelling on other peoples' past mistakes?"

At my uncle's house that day, summer had just begun, and it felt like it would never end. When I was younger, before we moved to California, I always knew exactly when the summer was over, when we were due to return to New York. My mother would start harvesting the last of the gerbera daisies, poppies, and chrysanthemums. All of the vases in the house would suddenly burst with red, orange, and gold, even in the bathrooms and the downstairs telephone alcove. We began visiting friends and neighbors with flowers in hand, saying our seasonal goodbyes. My grandmother would begin counting the days until my mother, the Math—if he'd flown out for the last two weeks of summer—and I would be leaving. Climbing into bed with Ojiichan and my grandmother early in the morning, I would make up ways that I could stay.

"Hide me in the chrysanthemums," I suggested, citing the tallest flowers in the garden, regal in their thickets. "No one would know, and Mom and Dad would leave without me."

"You have to go back home," she said in Japanese.

"I could hide," I said.

"Hiding is a poor way to live a life." My grandmother smiled automatically, and said, "Nobody gets to hide from what they belong to, and what belongs to them."

"What do you mean?" I asked, and she shook her head.

"You'll see," she told me, swinging her legs over the edge of the bed to start her day. She began to do her range of motion exercises. "It's something you learn more about later on."

I knew it was the end of summer when my mother drove all the way to Watsonville to shop at a specialty seed store to buy the same seven kinds of seeds: maiden flower, pampas grass, kudzu, fringed pink, and bush clover, ague, and balloon flowers. Most of these aren't even flowers, but straggly greens. One of them, maiden flower, smells so bad that it can't be in the house, or the room it's in will reek for a week. They're lonely, radiant blossoms and grasses. My mother planted them for my grandmother, never caring for their blandness herself. She far preferred the deep and wild banks of peonies and irises that had tangled side by side bordering the veranda, or the orchids that began their lives protected by her special lights and stubborn certainty that they would grow, or her white roses, even though the latter stuck her hands through her gloves and made her bleed.

Until my grandmother died, I never saw the seven flowers as anything but seeds in musty envelopes, the old shop proprietor's notes of name and cost scrawled across the envelope tops in smudgy pencil. Every year, we returned to New York before they bloomed. Planting them was our own private Labor Day.

My mother and I didn't speak as we worked, and maybe that's why she seemed then like someone whom I could know, and like. In Japanese, that kind of silence is called *haragei*, "belly language." One of my grandmother's friends came to call while my grandmother was sick with cancer. My mother helped my grandmother put on her makeup and the wig she needed after the effects of chemotherapy had set in. My grandmother and her friend sat on the veranda, facing each other but not speaking, until dusk. My mother served tea, and left them alone. Uncle Mas went home for dinner, and still they sat. I asked my mother if they were praying, and she said no.

"Sometimes people can communicate better without speech," she said, cleaning up after Uncle Mas. She rinsed his tea cup, and set it on the drainboard.

"What do you mean?" I asked.

"Language itself is deceptive. Language is a difficult thing."

"How?"

"You ask too many questions. Anybody can talk," she said irritably, as though we were speaking of teaching bears to dance. "Unfortunately, few ever truly learn."

Hara means "belly," or "gut," the wellspring of wishes, desires, and feelings. *Hara* figures vitally in the

Japanese view of human interaction. When people are angry, it's described as *hara ga tatsu*, "their bellies stand up." People who have a tacit agreement *hara o awaseru*, "put their bellies together." *Harakiri* means "to commit suicide," or literally, "to slit your own belly."

But my favorite was always *hara wa karimono*, which is what my grandmother used to say when she talked about babies, any babies, but especially her own. "*Hara wa karimono*," she would say, a faraway light soft in her eyes. "The womb is a borrowed thing."

In borrowing my mother's womb, I have the opportunity to borrow her standards. Not that any balanced person would. "Never accept a gift from a man, lest you be compromised." "If you can't think of anything nice to say, don't say anything at all." "Stop being mad, no one likes anyone who's mad." "Learning to listen will save you loneliness; men love to be listened to." "Don't question your elders and betters." (Practically everybody.) "Smile!"

My mother is beautiful. She has a heavy-lidded gaze, like the actress for whom she was named. When World War Two broke out, there was a feature in *Life* magazine on anatomical discrepancies between the Japanese and Chinese. The article was titled, "How to Tell a Jap from Your Friend." Uncle Sen has a copy of it in his home office. He collects camp memorabilia, putting up framed advertisements for "Jap Hunting Licenses Sold Here," "Sold Here" crossed out, and written instead, "*Free!*" My mother calls this the Wall of Shame.

Most Chinese have eyelids; Japanese don't. During the war and even afterward, the races were identified by their epicanthic folds, or lack thereof. My mother has a catching face by any standard, but after three major wars in the Pacific and an American cultural agenda that portrays Asian women as compliant geishas, she's a beautiful woman yoked by social stigma.

When I was small, my parents owned a Nikon and a Polaroid, so there are plenty of baby pictures of me, but the Swan Girls have carried on the family tradition their fathers began with my mother, telling me that I must have been adopted. Every July, the Swan Girls and I used to dress up in multilayered kimonos to attend *Obon*, the traditional summertime dance held at the Buddhist church. Practice held every night for two weeks prior to the dance. On the big night, the Swan Girls looked pristine and elegant, immaculately bound up in silk, subservience, and tradition. The obi around my waist squeezed the air out of me, and my feet were crammed into toe socks and Japanese slippers that seemed sized from small to tiny. Snowcone stains streaked the front of my kimono, I inevitably broke my fan by playing with it, and, sitting out the dances I didn't know, I perched on the edge of my chair, feet wide apart, like a basketball player waiting to be called into the game.

Once on the way home in the car, my grandmother tried to help me by telling me that I was *sabi*. *Sabi* is a Japanese ideology, originally a Buddhist one, wherein aesthetic pleasure is taken in the modest or awkward. *Sabishii* means "lonely." Defined by *sabi*, the lonely and desolate are believed to be beautiful.

Wabi is similar to *sabi*, in that it describes a life of peace and comfort found in the austere. It's the antithesis of "a chicken in every pot." According to Ojiichan, it's "a human in every coop, and liking it." My uncles and my mother have a deep horror of *wabi*, and so did Oji-ichan. "*Wabi*," he snorted, "is 'zact opposite of American Dream."

If *wabi* is the opposite of the American Dream, my mother is the embodiment of it. She learned to use her femininity and powerlessness to her advantage, and what should have been just her icing, fragile and sweet, became her armor instead. Materially and socially, she had an easier time growing up than her brothers did. In accordance with the candy-colored, big-finned ideals of her generation, the same boy who would follow my mother home from school begging for a date would beat up Uncles Sen and Wes for being Japanese.

Times change, and I lack her armor anyway. As a result, I understand her a little better than she understands me. A girl in New York once asked me, "How can you see out of that kind of eyes?" I told her that no matter what they looked like, I saw just the same from my eyes as she did from hers. Still, even back then, behind my invisible epicanthic folds of rice paper and Oriental silk, I knew that that wasn't so. And it never would be, any more than I would ever let my un-Cinderella-like Ugly-Stepsister feet be bound by my mother, or allow my mouth to become small and condensed in my face, only able to make a helpless twitter commonly associated with broken birds.

My mother rarely speaks in public, and for a beautiful brown-eyed woman, she has a stone cold gaze. Only the dumbest or the neediest would dare approach her on the street. Her concept of history is last week's shopping list. Local gossip heard at the church and grocery aside, people

and their motivations don't interest her, though she's as-
tute enough to know that they interest me. When the ex
and I were having problems but not yet fighting with each
other over who got to throw in the towel first, she asked
me one day over the phone, "Wil, do you ever talk about
ideas with him, or do you just talk about things?"

As with many comments from my mother, this came
out of nowhere. "I don't know," I said finally, helpless.
"I don't know what you mean."

"I asked if you ever share your ideas with him." Her
voice, kinder than the one she uses in public but still ut-
terly without warmth, grew vague. "You've always been
a girl with a lot of ideas," she said. She said this as though
it was a bad thing, as though she had never had an idea
or impulse in her life.

Maybe it was true. My mother gardens. Barring
beauty, that's her one true gift. Now that the Math is
frequently away on consulting jobs and I'm gone at university, she sometimes talks about starting a flower business, or a gardening service, but she's never serious. Partly
it's because Uncle Sen hoots derisively at her for wanting
to do what thousands of Japanese broke their backs doing
to save money before the war. And in his way, the Math
lets it be known that he would prefer that my mother not
allow gardening to grow beyond its present stage as rec-
reation and hobby.

She lacks the confidence to make it work because the
men in our family have delivered their verdict, and besides, to pursue what she desires would be the epitome of
everything she was raised to think of as crass and needless
for women: aggression, independence, even success. Still,
she loves flowers, and can make anything green grow. She

inherited that ability from her mother, along with definite eyelids, a wooden tongue for languages, and an aversion to the truth that may prove fatal, the same as it did for her mother. Early on, my grandmother contracted cancer of the truth. Then, things got really bad.

Honky Inferno

By dinnertime, the Schraders' house sparkles with shiny surfaces and polished glass illumined by dusk's orange light. The paperboy comes late, a laconic teen on a mountain bike. I collect the evening newspaper from the bottom of the drive, mindful that it's the last time I'll do this here. Across the street, doing the same thing, the neighbor waves to me. "Be sure to come by in the fall, for apple strudel," she calls. She cares deeply about the maintenance of her identity as an East Coast expatriate, Daughter of the American Revolution, and PCU faculty wife. Before I can compose a reply, a car comes toward me, headlights splashing on bits of glass from past errors in judgment along this twisty road.

Walking back to the house, I look toward the lights of PCU. Three years ago, I unwittingly arrived in Hell disguised as a college campus. In the beginning, ten thousand Liberal Zombies sucking psychocandies and attending placard-making parties seemed like the normal college experience. Then things began to go awry. For example, practically everybody at PCU is white. In a statistical release that had the Zombies picketing the administration complex for weeks, the state education department announced that PCU has the lowest minority count of all California public universities. That's not good for a campus that so piously points to its funds-gobbling multiculturalist program at annual budget appropriation meetings, but American universities are primarily white places. On the PCU application, twenty-seven different boxes to check under "Ethnic Identity" aside, we're known as minorities for a reason.

Yet somehow, it's always the white people scuttling around to ensure that everything is PC and proper, and raising a tremendous fuss when it isn't. Commitment to change, even when steeped in self-righteousness, can be admirable. Except that the PCU plan to solve moral grievances usually has to do with beer, drugs, and/or outmarrying after graduation. The Zombies support anyone and anything that hints of rights being infringed upon. This includes all-beef patties. As the poster says, "It's your lunch, but it's a cow's life."

Youthful earnestness has a stench like summertime roadkill. A Native American man told me it's my responsibility to educate others about the plight of my people. Does this mean responding soberly when Zombies are compelled to tell me the second they meet me that their best friends are Asian-Pacific-Islander American, and that they love sushi and rice? They want to know what my grandparents' concentration camp experience was like. They want to bond, to share how I feel. Only a Zombie would have the nerve to ask a total stranger to share their racial experience in the name of education, like they've missed the notes for some seminar.

Liberal Zombies believe that protest, passion, and hand-held microphones are the answer to every social ill. Empathy terrorists, their greatest strength lies in collective weakness. The outbreak of the Gulf War was the worst. REM's "It's the End of the World As We Know It" played for twenty-four hours straight. In preparation for Armageddon, the students shut down the school. I guess nobody wanted to miss the Two-Day Kegger Against Armageddon. A makeshift platform was set up in the bookstore parking lot, across from my dormitory. Not only could protestors there hear in pukey sonnet form why a fat, sulky poetry major from Iowa thinks war is a Bad Thing, checks could be made payable to the Enviromens' Coalition for a Better Planet, the campus group of profeminist men for the environment.

The entire male population at PCU was ready to caravan to Mexico. I told the ex I recommended bottled water, but couldn't condone Mexico. "Who asked you to?" snarled Mr. Charm. We were at the Armageddon party. A band was playing. People were dancing. It was the second night of the war, and the parking lot was alight with torches, flashlights, copies of the Constitution and the American flag in flames. The ex worked his lighter. He called me politically naive, and told me to grow up. Grow up and move to Mexico? Maybe the reason he never thought I had a sense of humor was because he had such a liberal one.

"You're lucky to have the opportunity to run to Mexico," I told him.

The flag in his hand blazing away, the ex sneered, "My parents wanted to name me Indiankiller, but got over their hippie guilt after naming my sister Khe Phang."

He doesn't have a sister. I can't look forward to going back to school, mostly because I don't want to see the ex. He's the press secretary for the Enviromens' Coalition. It's the most popular group on campus, in large part because they have the best parties, with the best girls: It might be PCU, but it's still college, twenty-year-olds shuffling haplessly on the self-devouring feed loop of youth. Last year an ordinance was passed banning looks discrimination, meaning the girl with the green hair and pierced lip has to be hired if she's qualified for the job. But unless the beer goggles are really fogging the old windows to the soul, all bets are off around the keg.

I tire of policing my language, and tire equally of dark imprecations muttered against people insensitive enough to fill up at Exxon, or shod their feet in Italian leather: Think globally, buy American! And then there are the cows again. Of course, it's a given that it's always white people nattering on in dire tones of wounded sanctimony both tragic and funny that they're sick, tired, and angry about inequality and unfairness among the races. It gets to be a bit much after a while. Most of the time I don't say anything, but I know it to be true: fairness and equality are two different things.

Growing up in a mecurial meritocracy, fairness and equality were scarce entities at best. Loosely grouped by age and interest, Grace, Joy, and Ashley were fierce rivals for attention, applause, love. Hope and Jennifer were pitted against one another from the start. The youngest girls, Faith, Katrina, and I were grouped together, except that I declined to compete, and Katrina died when she was ten, so Faith won.

Summers, we swam a lot. Grace went on to swim on the high school varsity team. The day of Katrina's accident, Grace, Joy, Hope, Faith, Ashley, Jennifer, Katrina, and I were playing Octopus, a game in which one person was the octopus and chased the others in the water. It was similar to Tag, except that the octopus caught and attached themselves to someone else. The object of the game then was basically to drown each other. Little finesse was required.

The day Katrina died, my mother was in Watsonville with my grandmother. Ojiichan was inside, taking a nap. Grace was in charge of all of us. Joy was wearing a bikini she didn't dare wear with our mothers around. She bought it from a friend. It looked like three pink dots held together by string. The transistor radio I'd just received for my birthday that year was playing bad seventies rock.

Hope was the octopus. First she chased Jennifer, who led her straight to Grace. Grace got out of the pool and ran into the house, which was cheating. Hope lunged, and started after Katrina and me. I dove under, thinking to propel myself underwater past the octopus. I held my breath and went all the way to the other side of the pool, which was why I missed what happened next.

When I surfaced in the shallow end, I heard Joy screaming for Grace, who came running out of the house. Katrina was sitting on the edge of the pool, her suit askew. There was blood and what I took for strings of sausages on the tile, and in the water. Hope, closest to Katrina, lifted herself out of the pool and started dragging Katrina back from the water. I couldn't understand why it was such a struggle for her. It looked like Katrina was in the middle of a game of tug-of-war. That was when I saw that Katrina had sat squarely on the pool vacuum right above one of the filters, and the grate was gone. Its suction had eviscerated her.

We liked to drop rocks into the vacuum to hear them sucked into the earth. My mother always warned us to keep long hair and towels away from the vacuum when it was on. She said she didn't want to have to call the pool man to clean the vacuum. Grace or Joy called 911. When they arrived, the paramedics kept telling us not to worry, that Katrina might make it. My mother and grandmother came home, and before they rushed off to the hospital, they both said it couldn't have been as bad as we said it was. My mother was so sure of this that she had time to notice Joy's racy little suit and tsk-tsk. But the Swan Girls and I accepted Katrina's death, if not easily, then immediately, without question. We had seen it, and had no need to rationalize what we had seen.

"They tried to make Katrina a new part from her own intestine," I heard The Math tell someone about the accident, "but she had lost too much blood." It was then that I realized Kiki had become Katrina. The pool was drained two months early that year. None of us went to Katrina's funeral.

After the accident, Uncle Sen and Aunt Ann sent Ashley and Jennifer away to school. They didn't even come back for our grandmother's funeral two years later. In frenzied compulsion, Uncle Sen started renovating the house, although he was never there to appreciate the fruits of the labors he paid for. Hardly a season went by that their place wasn't in complete disarray. Where her *kokeshi* collection had once been a hobby leftover from her childhood, Aunt Ann began accumulating the dolls with an aggressiveness that made everyone uneasy, foreign as it was to her languorous pre-Katrina née Kiki demeanor. Ashley ceased all contact with us, even with Grace, her closest friend in the family. Grace swam, but it was no longer for fun. Throughout high school she competed up and down the state. None of the family attended the weekend meets, but the trophies accumulated on Grace's dresser, eventually shelved at the ranch. Hope stopped swimming completely and took up knitting, macramé, needlepoint. Sometimes she sat with my grandmother on the porch, an adolescent Arachne, working and worrying yarn, cord, string until it had shape and meaning. Joy became more nasty than ever, picking on everybody younger than her, the ringleader of a merciless social clique at school wherein, if an outcast, Joy personally saw to it that life was Hell. Faith stayed as close to home as possible, becoming docile to the extreme, the baby of the family.

She, and everyone else, ceased to speak of Kiki. When they did, it was made clear that Katrina had died unexpectedly, but peacefully. Often, I heard the accident termed as a fatal head injury, as though she had slipped and fallen by the side of the pool.

Thus, nobody blamed anybody, and nobody got angry. But now nobody can keep the history straight either. Everyone has their own interpretation of the family and their place in it. We repeat the same stories about ourselves and one another over and over again, stories that haven't gained power and definition in the telling, but have lost it.

We hear about how Uncle Mas severed his thumb with the weed whacker. First, he hosed off the whacking part of the weed whacker, because dried blood on nylon is hard to clean. Then he found his thumb in the lawn, packed it in ice, showered, changed, and drove himself to the hospital, where the appendage was taken from the Coleman cooler Uncle Mas had packed it in and was reattached. Then he drove home. He didn't say anything about it to anybody; it was two or three weeks before my grandmother noticed that the bloody gauze on Uncle Mas's left hand seemed to be a long-term thing.

We're told that when Uncle Sen and Aunt Ann met, he was one of five suitors for her hand in marriage. She narrowed the field to two, Uncle Sen and another guy, but still couldn't decide. One afternoon Uncle Sen drove up to her parents' house and saw his competitor's car parked on the sloped road. He let out the parking brake, and gave the car a push. The owner of the car ran out of the house, screaming and cursing. Aunt Ann and her sisters crowded onto the lawn to see. The car plowed into a tree at the bottom of the hill. Uncle Sen brought out a one-carat pear-shaped diamond he had borrowed money from

Ojiichan to buy, and he and Aunt Ann were married that summer.

We see that as openly combative as Uncle Sen is, Uncle Wes is Zen and passive. When he was just home from Vietnam, he was driving to San Francisco when two men got into his pickup cab at the stoplight before the highway. Nobody said a word, and they drove three abreast for two hours. Once they arrived in the city, Uncle Wes asked the hitchhikers if they needed to go anyplace in particular. They answered in the negative, thanked him, and got out at the next stoplight.

We find out that my mother was such a terrible student, she drove around with her typewriter in the trunk of her car so she could whip up papers in the parking lot before class.

We talk about how Ojiichan learned English by reading the Constitution, and how my grandmother forecasted her own death forty years in advance. Still, to my mother and her brothers and my cousins, these are distant fables, tedious, occasionally charming, but not relevant to our lives today.

My grandmother never discussed her past between her girlhood in Japan and life at the ranch, which Ojiichan bought ten years after America's wartime law barring Japanese from becoming citizens was repealed. Nor did my grandmother ever mention her employer, Ann Sayles, now in her late eighties. My grandmother cleaned the Sayles' house, and cooked dinner for Reg and Ann and their two girls. She did this up until the war, and then after, until she and Ojiichan had saved enough money to buy Uncle Mas his house. My mother still takes flowers to Ann Sayles, does her grocery shopping on occasion, and remembers her on her birthday and at Christmas. In return, Ann Sayles reminds my mother and me that back in the war days, Japanese were the Yellow Peril and nobody would hire them. Ann Sayles had taken a big social risk with my grandmother: I loathe peer pressure, my dear. I even hired your grandfather to do the orchard and paint the garage.

She says my grandmother was the best worker she's ever had, not like the Southeast Asian girls she's been forced to hire of late. But my grandmother, she was so cute, not knowing how the toaster worked, and what it was for. She had never had bread before she got to America. Excepting the brief influence of fifteenth century Portuguese missionaries, bread, butter, and chocolate weren't introduced to the common Japanese populace until the occupying forces had landed some twenty years after my grandmother had left.

Ann Sayles talks about the war, and my grandmother. She was heartbroken when a few bad apples spoiled it for everybody, and the Japanese all got carted off to internment camps. "What bad apples?" I demanded. We were having tea at the Sayles' house, the same old rambling gingerbread in the hills that my grandmother had once taken care of. My mother kicked me in the ankle.

"The ones on the fishing boats, my dear," Ann Sayles said, clearly mystified that I didn't know. "The ones passing codes to the Japanese in your homeland."

No wonder my grandmother never talked about Ann Sayles. By the time I came along, my grandmother had completely blocked out the middle of her life, between childhood and the cusp of death. As far as she was concerned, it was at the spacious ranch house that she reinhabited her life. Having survived, she wasn't interested in the analysis of her survival via the telling of her war stories to us. It would have been like trying to verbalize what it had been to experience a miracle to a bunch of heathens.

One New Year's Eve, we were all together and Uncle Sen, drunk, made a joke about living in a chicken coop when they first returned to California, after the war. My grandmother cocked her head.

"What chicken coop?" she asked.

"Have some more sashimi, fresh from Hawaii," my mother suggested, an unsubtle nudge toward the family's present prosperity in contrast with what once was—and toward changing the subject.

Uncle Sen swilled his drink around in his glass. "The one we all lived in, behind Pop's Bedbug Hostel," he said easily. He always referred to Ojiichan's Esperanza by that name, and until I knew what a hostel was, I heard it as Bedbug Hostile. It seemed accurate to me.

"It had dirt floors," Uncle Sen went on, "and a shit-covered hen house where we broiled in the summer, and froze in the winter."

"Sen," my mother said.

"Excuse me, Ava," he amended with faux chivalry. He bolted the rest of his drink down the hatch. "We would have frozen, but the chickens slept with us, the chickens and the ticks and the fleas. My view is," he concluded, although nobody had asked for his view; actually, everyone looked like they'd rather he'd shut up, "if it looks like a chicken, smells like a chicken, and clucks like a chicken . . ."

Here, he stuffed his hands in his armpits, flapped, and let out a deafening squawk more suggestive of rage than chicken. The Swan Girls and I didn't agree on much, but there was a consensus that Uncle Sen was weird. He was laughing and joking and pulling twenty dollar bills out of our ears one minute, perched at the preverbal apex of ornithological horror to rival Hitchcock the next. Discounting my mother's disgust, which was perpetual where Uncle Sen was concerned, nobody reacted. My grandmother struck him over the nose with her chopsticks. Then she offered the teriyaki sirloin around again.

But sometimes Uncle Sen kept it up until somebody snapped, and history, always the same history, spewed forth in a noxious torrent: How the FBI picked Ojiichan up right after Pearl Harbor, and for a year, nobody even knew where he was. My grandmother sold the radio, the good rugs, everything they owned. Strangers came right to the door to inquire about china, silver, the car. Uncle Mas, acting as head of the household at fourteen, refused to sell the car to a man who offered twenty dollars for it. That night, the car was stolen out of the driveway. Forty years and numerous cars later, Uncle Mas still gets a hangdog look on his face when the old Model T is mentioned. Yet at the time, they counted themselves lucky. Their friends the Okados' house was burned to the ground.

The Japanese were kept at a converted race track until they were sent away. At the train station, a white girl about Uncle Mas's age spit on him. The rumor was that the Japanese would be sent back to Japan, a country that meant nothing to my uncles, who believed themselves to be Americans good as any other, if not better, because they had been tested and appreciated it more.

They still do, in their own weary way. Years later, talking about Japan-bashing at a typical family dinner, Uncle Wes expressed himself like this: "We couldn't live how we do anywhere else, but even fifty years later, 'A Jap is a Jap,' fer Chrissake. Pass the spuds, Ava."

"Except at PCU," I reminded him, taking the bowl from my mother. "At PCU, a Jap might conceivably be an Asian-Pacific-Islander American."

"God. Here," my mother said, handing me the salt.

"That place," the Math snorted, forking his pork chop. "Well, I hear valets make pretty good tips."

"Bah," Uncle Sen grumped at his end of the table. He had long ago dispensed with eating, and now just drank. He had lost a lot of weight, and meeting his eyes was like being stared down by death. "Bedwetting Bolsheviks."

"Bastion of barbarians," the Math agreed, taking up the conversation's alliterative theme.

"Better dead than Red, fer Chrissake," Uncle Wes added, snowing his potatoes with salt until they looked like the Alps of high blood pressure sitting on his plate. "Prefer 'Jap' to Island Whatever. Right, Masa?"

"Rice," grunted Uncle Mas, pointing with his eyes.

ARMS Control

My grandparents both used to say it, and my parents, uncles, and aunts still do. Everybody believes I need to suffer more. And not just me; whenever the elder members of the family get together, by the time dessert and tea rolls around, talk inevitably turns to the worrisome decline of quality suffering in the lives of their offspring.

They agree that even if it has to be purchased to be had, everyone needs to suffer. I despise being told I haven't suffered enough. I can't understand why, when my grandmother was so religious and my mother and her brothers worked so hard to put past adversities behind them, they're so anxious about their young peoples' lack of hardship. When she goes on about it, I tell my mother that with all that's wrong in the world, I think she should sit back, relax, and let Buddha handle the suffering.

In the car, driving to the ranch from the Schraders' house, my mother starts complaining about suffering. First, Uncle Mas, who is called Masa by his brothers and sister. His full name is a real tongue-twister, Masahiro Yoshigeteru. My mother is sure that with all the Spam he eats, his cholesterol level is about nine hundred and four. She wishes she knew for sure, but since his heart attack and quadruple bypass five years ago, he's been to the doctor maybe twice, and one time was to get a wart burned off the back of his hand.

Aunt Em is fed up with him. He spends most days at the ranch, helping my mother around the house or watching TV. One day last week, Aunt Em came over while Uncle Mas was out buying lottery tickets, and apologized for the canyonlike indentation he was making on my mother's couch.

As I often do with my mother, I strive for the noncommittal. "Aunt Em tries hard," I observe.

"Tries hard, doing what? Ruin his life?" In her agitation, we almost tour the ditch by the side of the road. A road marker kisses the front fender in the dark. I'm trying to pry my fingernails out of the dashboard, but my mother doesn't seem to notice. "I told her, the whole thing, I *oshimimasu*," my mother tells me. She always speaks Japanese to Aunt Em. "*Oshimimasu*" is an automatic insult because it means both to regret and to deplore. My mother disburses diplomacy selectively. A good rule of thumb is, the less well she knows a person, the better she behaves. Unfortunately, the converse results that ensue from this equation are exactly what one would imagine them to be.

"Poor Masa," she continues. "Grace not married, and so old."

"You should wait until she's on the dark side of thirty to pass your judgment," I say, knowing that even this is impossible.

"Don't have to wait long. Hope, turning her back on her family. Faith, I don't know, child development?" My mother frowns. "Good university, but what kind of study is that?"

My mother would never cite Uncle Mas's second daughter, Joy, as a link in her father's chain of pain. Joy is to all of them what her name indicates. Husband, two children, split level by a man-made lake that's sinking an inch every year.

"So they're happy," I say. "They found their freedom."

"Freedom! His whole family, like a conspiracy." She grimaces at their spitefulness. "Especially Hope. She broke her parents' hearts, going crazy at college the way she did."

As time passes, myth is slowly coagulating around the younger generation. Grace can't find a decent man to date, let alone marry. She was once stood up on a blind date because the guy was taken to jail that afternoon, charged with assault with a deadly weapon and intent to kill. He phoned her later, from prison, but she remained unimpressed.

Jennifer was a mouthy teenage rebel child who once gave her father, Uncle Sen, a flock of ten hens for his birthday. We had fresh eggs at the ranch until the chickens all died one by one. Sarcasm was de rigeur. Home for the holidays one Christmas she asked him how his alcoholism was coming along. He menaced her from his Barcalounger. Jennifer charged him and pushed the chair over backwards with him in it, then ran out the door. She eventually married a Chinese trial lawyer in San Francisco. All vestiges of youthful insurgency have vanished behind her matronly mien.

Something went horribly awry with Hope at college, where she met Avery Jones and, apparently swept up by love, ran away with him after he graduated to live in Sin. Now they live in a cramped flat somewhere in the city. Though disowned, Hope recently tried to get her hands on a small inheritance left her by her maternal grandfather in Japan. Uncle Mas was inclined to let her have it, but, punishing through the pocketbook, Aunt Em said no.

Regarding Hope, I tell my mother, "That's not what happened. She didn't go crazy."

"Oh? What happened?"

"I'm just saying, you might not know."

She goes right on. "They told her not to do it, and she did anyway. Aunt Em told her, get married, and if you don't like each other, who cares, get divorced!"

I goggle anew. "That makes sense to you?"

"Sure! What kind of daughter is that," she asks me, "who doesn't love her parents? She turned out so undutiful!" Here we go: duty. According to my mother, it isn't love that makes the world go 'round. "Hope said she had to be free. Free! All you young people, so concerned with your freedom, never think ahead. You do what you want, don't care about anybody else, what people say to us."

"You must have unusually inconsiderate friends."

"*Ishiatama*," she snorts. Literally, this means, "rock-head." She seems to be referring to her rockhead, free-dom-fighter nieces and daughter rather than to her rockhead friends. "So embarrassing. It looks like we don't know how to control all of you. Uncle Mas was a virgin until he was thirty," she appends suddenly.

"I remember."

"I think, this happens because you have too much freedom," she lets me know. "If you had more *kurush-imi*," painful experience that does you good, "you would know better the hurt you cause, running after freedom. Then you know consequence."

"You don't know all of Hope's experiences."

"Nothing compared to some people," my mother says vehemently, expelling one of the cornerstones of her "I'm OK, you I'm not sure about" guide to life like a big dogma hairball.

"Suffering is individual, not relative."

But in this family, suffering certainly is *relatives*. My mother goes on to Uncle Sen, who has eczema all over his body. Aunt Ann is considering leaving him, a trial separation. Aesthetics are a chronic concern with Aunt Ann, but mostly it's Uncle Sen's conduct of late that has her hide chapped. My mother hopes to go to their continually metamorphosing house and talk her into staying with Uncle Sen. Aunt Ann went straight from being Miss Peach Pit in 1910 or whenever to being Uncle Sen's wife, and her Peach Pit days are long gone.

"Like she would ever leave him," I scoff, even as I feel a feminist twinge. Still, this is Aunt Ann we're talking about, the woman who adds one and one together and comes up with three every time.

"When you bring suffering upon yourself, that's really terrible," my mother says disapprovingly.

"Uncle Sen is a jerk," I agree.

"So disrespectful, you," she complains, agitation refreshed by my remark. "I thought I raised you better, but I guess I'm wrong about that."

I shrug, mad at her, thinking, You think you know everybody's *kurushimi*, but you don't. My mother believes that too much freedom ruins a person, but not enough can be even worse. Instead of promising to buy her a new car at graduation if she was good throughout high school, Hope's parents should have let her drive the family car around first, letting her get accustomed to the idea of independence. When Hope went to college, she started drinking. She couldn't hold alcohol, turning crimson after half a beer. In this family, all the enzymes that break down alcohol went straight to Uncle Sen.

There was a guy Hope liked. She thought he was okay, because he knew Jennifer from summer camp. He told Hope she was much prettier than Jennifer, and nicer, too. Hope and Jennifer had always been competitors, and his opinions pleased Hope very much.

He raped her in her dorm room one night after a party. They had both been drinking. One hundred other people around, neighbors up and down, fore and aft, and she didn't scream. She didn't struggle, she just kept saying No, and she didn't even say that when he took a stuffed animal before he left. He said he wanted a souvenir.

I sit beside my mother in the dark, in the car, and

listen to her talk about suffering. My mother laments the suffering Aunt Ann's instability causes Uncle Sen, and that Aunt Em and Hope cause Uncle Mas. I bet even if she knew the other side of the story, she'd side with her brothers. Hope never reported the rape because then her family would know. She could already hear her father muttering, "Stupid." People don't handle randomness well. Everything has to have a cause, a reason why it happened, or else it could happen to you.

What about the suffering Hope was caused by being raised in a household where her father never speaks, yet it's the women who have no voice? My mother doesn't see that Avery isn't what made Hope crazy at college; he *kept* her from going crazy there. Hope couldn't eat or sleep, and she was put on academic probation. It was Avery who got Hope to an OBGyn for the first time in her life. Hope didn't even know what OBGyn was an acronym for. We were told nothing about our bodies. My mother said tampons wouldn't fit until I was married, but didn't explain why.

I sit with my hands each captured in the other, listening to her speak. She thinks she knows everything. Steering our way home conversationally via neutral topics of discussion, it occurs to me that my mother doesn't know how I suffer, silently listening to her talk about Joy's new baby. She doesn't mention the ex, but not out of deference to me or my feelings. She has no idea that my heart wasn't broken by the ex once, but twice. The second time was worse. Joy's baby looks more like Joy every day. My mother says that boys born first in the birth order look like the mother's family, first girls like the father's. Second sons are the reverse. And if the first two children are the same sex, the second one will be taller. I'd love to ask my mother how abortion factors into her tidy birth order equations but quell myself in time.

My mother is full of facts like these. She says that I have a commonplace birthday, born in the ninth month on the second day in seventy-two. With the exception of seven, odd numbers are considered lucky, and three and five are regarded as especially good. Nothing in my birthdate even adds up to three or five. My mother always points this out in a faintly accusatory way, though she had more to do with this calamity than I did. Might as well blame the stork, Mom. She says that I was overdue, and she was afraid I'd be born on the fourth. Four is the unluckiest number in the Japanese lexicon, "four" in Japanese being written as "*shi*," which also means death.

"People with 'four' birthdays have a hard time," my mother always says reflectively. "They suffer more in life."

"Heck," I murmur, "I'd think the Japanese would love that."

When I was small, I asked my grandmother, "How do you make a bird sing?" She quoted an old Japanese parable. "Nobunaga says, 'Kill it!' Hideyoshi says, 'Make it want to sing.' Ieyasu says, 'Wait.' "

My grandmother always made me want to sing. As a child, I disliked milk, and my mother worried I wouldn't grow. After one of her trips to Japan, my grandmother brought back a new drinking cup for me. It was pale blue glass, with hand-painted *sakura*, cherry blossoms, dancing around the rim. Etched beneath the cherry blossoms was a caption that read, "Dream Cup: Sip your Dreams by Drops." My grandmother vowed that this cup had the power to transform ordinary liquids into magical elixirs. I loved the idea of sipping my dreams by drops. I drank a lot of milk thereafter, and in this way, I grew tall. At one point, my grandmother said that if the unthinkable happened and I grew more, I'd never find a Japanese man to marry because they all wanted wives shorter than themselves. I didn't get the chance to prove her wrong about this—she died when I was five foot two.

Born and raised in Japan, my grandmother always upheld the feudal metaphors associated with cherry blossoms. She believed in the transitory nature of life, harsh beauty found in death. She used to say that time is a wheel. I never knew what she meant. I pictured a wagon wheel rotating past skulls and tumbleweeds in a barren boneyard. Sometimes, I pictured the dharma wheel that adorns the front doors of the Buddhist church, the wheel with which every Sunday, Reverend Matsunaga attempts to steer his congregation closer to Nirvana. The wheel turns, your grandparents die, your parents die, until you're at the top, rolling alone toward what is both the most straightforward and the most obscure threshold humans ever can know.

My grandmother claimed she always knew what she would die of, she just didn't know when it would happen. Sitting on the veranda, a short while away from permanent collapse on the hospital bed set up in the living room, my grandmother told me what nobody else believed. She said she felt she had cancer before the doctors told her she did. She'd always known she wouldn't live long, and here she was, barely sixty years old, fighting for breath like a fish out of water.

Before her self-diagnosis, she had never been sick a day in her life, and upon hearing her prophecy, everybody laughed at her.

"Old woman," Ojiichan said, and got to shaking his head and laughing so hard, he couldn't finish. He never called her by name. He addressed her as "old woman" or "*oi*," "Hey, you." She referred to him as "*ano hito*," "that person." Still sniggering to himself, Ojiichan walked out of the hospital room to the park across the street, where Uncle Wes found him at nightfall, staring at his scarred hands, fingers yellow with nicotine.

Ojiichan called it hoker poker. My mother told my grandmother not to talk about this to anyone outside the family. Uncle Sen asked the doctor about chemotherapy's effects on lucidity. The Math tried to explain to my grandmother the illogic of her premonition from a biological perspective, to no avail. She felt her disease in her lungs. She knew she didn't have long to live.

Nobody disputed the latter. My mother related the goings-on to Reverend Matsunaga. He came by one day shortly thereafter, and dropped off several tapes of his sermons and chants. From then on it became his habit to stop in a few times a week to collect the old tapes and drop off the new. This sense of urgency in an older gentleman usually so celestially serene he appeared to be tranquilized indicated to my mother that the tapes might save my grandmother from her disease. In the end, however, there was no epiphany and no reversal, and my grand-mother simply died.

"I don't know how Grandma knew she was going to die," I tell my mother as we pull into the driveway of the ranch.

"What made you think that?"

"I don't know." I don't tell her that I associate the place with the event: returning to the ranch is like returning to the beginning of a bad dream. I can't see anything in the dark, but it's a place of nightmares none-theless. Late summer cicadas sing their annual dirge in the garden. I might disdain the knowledge, but I know everything about this place as though it's engraved on an internal template from which all that I say and do originates.

"Who said she knew?" My mother suddenly hits the brakes. "Look at the fat badger," she says, pointing into the darkness.

"Where?" The car leaps right and forward, head-lights splashing wildly. "Oh, I see," I say quickly, trying not to clutch at the seat.

Our headlights catch the eyes of a murky shadow hurrying toward the garden. "Look at him," my mother gripes, "on his way to dinner." She beeps the car horn in frustration. For all her unpredictability, there have been certain cadences to my mother's rhythm through life. She's pragmatic to the point of cruelty, a cool customer where matters of the heart are concerned. I study her dashboard-lit profile in its vampirical elegance, and she turns toward me, brow in a ball. "What?"

I touch my throat, say, "I thought you set out traps."

"Badgers are too smart for gopher traps."

We motor slowly past the house. No lights on, but the Math is probably home. "Grandma said she knew she was going to die," I tell my mother, to get her back on track.

"I guess she just had a feeling," she says reluctantly.

No wonder everyone was thrown. This group wouldn't know a feeling if it bit them in the butt. "Everyone thought she was a victim of second-hand smoke," I remember aloud.

"Of course," my mother dismisses, surprising me.

"Really?"

She shrugs again, tapping the garage remote. "She was shrouded in smoke all the time, Ojiichan's cigarettes, your uncles', everybody's. That's what caused her cancer, among other things."

"What other things?"

"Other things."

"Like what?" I persist.

She frowns, parks the car in the garage before answering. "Fifty years in a country she could never show her true self in, couldn't breathe the air of without reserve? After she left Japan, she never breathed properly again."

"She lacked freedom," I encapsulize with relish, prematurely enjoying the cyclical nature of this conversation.

"Real freedom is freedom from choice," my mother opines coldly. "Everybody knows that."

"She didn't have to marry Ojiichan," I suggest. My grandmother's father had promised her to Ojiichan when she was a little girl. If her father hadn't died when she was small, it might've been different. As it was, he thought he'd scored a coup, promising his older daughter to the only son of people of some substance. My grandmother's father couldn't have known Ojiichan would decide to come to America.

"Of course she had to marry him," my mother says, really chapped now. "Coming here, Ojiichan gave everything to the natural brother, already married. And Mama's mother couldn't change her late husband's decision, or else he would have lost face."

"Posthumously?" I ask.

"The Buddhists say, it's just one life," my mother intones in a reflective manner that hints of other chances rich in texture and scope. These opportunities shimmer beyond where ignorant third-generation eyes can see.

"Great." I sound petulant, disappointed by my shortcomings in the divination arena and my grandmother's big gyp. Her father couldn't lose face, so she lost her life. "It doesn't seem fair." My mother looks at me like I've just said the dumbest thing she's ever heard.

"Why should life be fair?" she asks, turning her face away from the automatic seatbelt buzzing past so that she's looking directly at me. "You need a haircut," she diagnoses. "I'll make an appointment tomorrow." Getting out of the car, she leans back in. "Did Faith tell you about your date? He sounds like a nice boy."

Life is getting more unfair by the minute. "I suppose you're going to tell me I have no choice," I whine, hating the way I sound when I speak to my mother.

"You're the one who's always talking about free-

dom," she says, and slams the car door. The engine ticks
as it cools. I exhale. It looks like I am home.

My grandmother's only dream was to return to Japan.
Instead, she died in a country she hated surrounded by
children and grandchildren she couldn't communicate with
in Japanese or in English because everybody spoke both
poorly, neither well. The moment before she died, she
turned her face away from her family as though finally able
to turn away from America as she'd wanted to do all
along.

After I was in the hospital, I started thinking a lot of
my grandmother. At the time of her death, I put her out
of my mind. Now I try to recall her and her Japanese
ways.

She would have said it was good that I was getting
my romantic suffering out of the way at a young age. It
polishes character and readies the sufferer for reality that
much earlier. She often said that the most dangerous thing
that can happen to a person is falling in love. The best
anyone can hope for in a relationship is mutual tolerance;
it's dangerous to require love as well.

My grandmother always said she hoped the man I
married would be tall. Height is a point of pride with
typically short Japanese Americans as it's a necessity in
looking down on others. My grandmother said that everybody has hopes, fears, fragilities, and dreams, but most
people have no one to share any of that with. Loneliness
is universal, not the property of any one culture or people.
Inner peace depends on loneliness being used for solitary
pleasure rather than lamented as undeserved tragedy.

Throughout their lives together, Ojiichan maligned

my grandmother for being weak, but she was strong enough to leave her family and country behind to marry a man she didn't know. She was strong enough to continue living afterward. She just couldn't keep her dreams alive, and, arguably her greatest shortcoming, she couldn't change her dreams once the old ones died. Obsolete pictures of possibilities as opposed to actualities depleted her strength, immobilizing her with fatalism, pessimism, and regret.

Discontent is immeasurable, largely because its only toll is in what never comes to pass. But people can let go and forget: Nobody wants to think they've missed out on anything potentially better than what they have or worse, realize that they've cheated themselves out of something better than what they've come to be content with, come to be lulled by.

As age encroaches on formerly immortal terrain, human beings suffer more and more literal and figurative death: job anxiety, money woes, marital problems, divorce, age itself. All of this allegorical loss is what I call ARMS, Acquired Rigor Mortis of the Soul. ARMS is the death of all dreams. I no longer sip my dreams by drops, but I still catch sight of them at the bottom of my glass, waiting for me. I'm just not sure how to get there from here. That was my grandmother's problem, too, and finally, she had to let go.

Hen and Chicks

~~~~~~~~

My bedroom at the ranch used to be my mother's bedroom. My grandmother had painted it pink for her. Ojiichan put in a free-standing rose quartz crystal he found on a rock expedition. My mother hung her jewelry on it, thin gold chains, friendship rings, her charm bracelet caught on sharp pink crags.

When I was in high school, the Math and Uncle Mas painted the room pale yellow, and my mother made new curtains. The ugly old linoleum was taken out, ecru carpet put in. With its eastern light, waking up in this room is like waking in the center of a daffodil.

The curtains are from China, previously a bolt of silk shantung from the family of one of Ojiichan's friends, an old man to whom my mother takes flowers and reads the Japanese-American newspaper, a stop on her weekly flower route, consisting of Ojiichan and my grandmother's friends, and Ann Sayles. The quilt that covers my bed was given to my mother by Ann Sayles, after she won it at a Buddhist church bazaar raffle my mother took her to. The quilt was once a study in pastel double wedding rings, but over the years, it's been sun-bleached to the same shade as the curtains and carpet.

Books and magazines line all four walls, neatly arranged on shelves the Math built. Organized alphabetically and chronologically, every issue of *Florist*, *Gourmet*, *Living*, *Sunset*, and *Traveler* ever printed is stored here. The Math's journals and readers are in boxes, and his books on strategy for everything from the stock market to cribbage are in rows. Published in 1971, *What to Name the Baby* is brown with age. Inside, "Emmett" and "William" are marked for a boy, "Daisy" and "Wilhelmina" for a girl. Names like Dean, Grace, Ken, and Joyce are popular with Japanese Americans. I've never met any Japanese Americans named Emmett or Wilhelmina.

Soil maps from the county surveyor's office and a collection of ranch photos shot from an aerial view are sandwiched between cookbooks and the childhood literature I left behind. Ojiichan's old mineralogy guides take up one whole wall. The Swan Girls and I used to look through these texts, enchanted by photos of cursed diamonds, minerals with the power to heal, and lowly stones. We knew the names of almost all the rocks we found on the ranch. Those we didn't, we invented names for, invariably ending in "ite." We discovered Hopeite, Faithite, Wilite, all magical stones with restorative powers. "Those just rocks," Ojiichan would snort, sitting on the veranda, watching us play. "That just gravel, nothing special."

The ranch is a fair-sized piece of property on the outskirts of a university town. Rumor is, despite the town's present no-growth status, the land will be rezoned for housing within the next decade. In the past five years, developers have begun coming around with increasing frequency. My mother serves them tea and asks the right questions while Uncle Mas sits nearby listening to the responses, to be commented on later, in private, with the Math. The ranch was divided into four shares amongst my mother and her brothers, but Uncle Sen relinquished claim on his quarter, and a few years ago, Uncle Wes sold his to Uncle Mas and my mother so the land would be protected from California community property law when he leaves Aunt May for good.

It's the next day, and my mother is expecting a developer from the city at noon. Uncle Mas comes over around ten-thirty, carrying an Idaho paper. He spots me, and nods. My mother asks him to check the badger traps she's assembled. They're lined up in the foyer, waiting to be set up outside. Uncle Mas does so, grunts approvingly, settles down at the kitchen table with the real estate section and a yellow highlighter. Since he retired, his dream has been to buy a summer retreat in Idaho. He goes up to look around, but hasn't found anything yet. He uses a magnifying glass to read the paper, holding the glass close to the page while leaning as far back as possible in his chair. He used to hold all reading material at arm's length, but in recent years his worsening eyesight has outdistanced his reach.

My mother sits across from him, holding her pen to

her cheek and gazing out the window. She's trying to think up the title for her garden club's entry into this year's state fair flower exhibit. Earlier, she was in and out of the house, tending to her huge pot of sweet relish, using the Schraders' tomatoes. The kitchen smells of sugar, cloves, and cooking vegetables. Up at dawn, my mother made breakfast, washed out her Mason jars, swept the kitchen floor, did a load of laundry and hung it out to dry, answered the phone three times, ran the vacuum around the living room, where the visiting developer will be entertained, ironed linens, got a tray and cups down from the Shaker cabinet in the dining room, and set up new badger traps. The traps are a loan from the manager of the country club golf course. Parts strewn on old newspapers spread over the kitchen floor, my mother labored over their assembly for almost an hour. She looked like Wile E Coyote with an Acme Company special delivery.

" 'We grow, therefore we are,' " she announces contemplatively. After a while, she checks her watch and gets up to take the traps outside and set them up. When she comes in, she washes her hands and starts braising chicken in garlic and oil for a soup base for lunch.

"This is Mama's recipe," she tells me. Then, "Wes dropped these pullets by," she divulges for Uncle Mas's benefit, expertly hacking one into eight neat pieces before dipping them in egg, flour, and spices. She tosses them into the pan of smoking oil and sizzling garlic. " 'Have some chicken, fer Chrissake,' he says. He stop at your place before he left, Masa?"

Uncle Mas shakes his head.

"Where'd he go?" I ask.

"Some lake, fishing trip. He shot these himself at

Clara's farm," my mother says. Back to the chickens. "Plucked and singed them for me, too. Did you hear, Clara's sold their place? They bought it in, what, Masa, twenty-five? No later than nineteen twenty-six I bet. Actually, Danny sold their place," my mother clarifies, referring to Clara Kanzaki's eldest son. "They bought it in Danny's name, because it was against the law for Japanese to own property, but Danny was an American citizen. If it was twenty-five, he was a toddler. Anyway, they bought it for five thousand dollars, sold it for half a million. Not bad."

"That's all?" Uncle Mas snorts.

"Bad economy now," my mother says.

"Danny, a fool," Uncle Mas diagnoses as an alternative explanation for the distress sale of the farm.

I take an apple from the larder. "How did they hold onto it during the war?"

My mother shrugs, chopping cilantro. "Left it with friends. Lucky, I guess. Danny and Carol are moving up to Oregon."

"Do you need any help?" I ask my mother.

"Set the table," she says. "Let's get lunch out of the way, I have things to do."

Uncle Mas eats very little stew, but consumes four bowls of rice. Due to a long-time digestive ailment, he subsists mainly on rice, liquids, and the occasional seed. The developer arrives at noon. Circumnavigating the living room by going through the dining room and kitchen, I peek in and see my mother attending to the lemon squeezer. When serving tea to white guests, she sets out lemon, cream, and sugar. I can see that the developer isn't only white, but a woman. Consequently, Uncle Mas looks like a flagpole was rammed down his neck into the back of his shirt. My mother is so nice to the visitor I can see the visitor relaxing, leaning back a little in her chair, having a second cup of tea.

"Wil," my mother says, spotting me. "Come meet Robin. She went to your same university."

I want to signal her to run. Instead, we shake hands. As I retreat into the kitchen, my mother follows me to get more hot water. "That shirt has a button missing," she hisses. "Sleeveless, that looks terrible."

"I wear this shirt a lot." I study my gingham self. "I've had it for years. You don't think it's good conservationism?"

She swills the kettle around, patting its side, to test the temperature of the water. "I think that's an insult to the poor."

Acquiescing to her displeasure, I go to change my shirt. I sink down on my bed for a moment. The pale gold warmth of the walls, the comfortable roughness of the quilt beneath me, the smell of detergent, sun, and faded book covers are all familiar in a way that makes me nostalgic and uneasy at the same time. Beneath my head, my pillow is still faintly damp, rather as though I cried in the night while I slept. Or maybe I just drooled a lot.

My grandmother died when I was twelve years old, and that year, for the first time, I was able to see the maiden flower, pampas grass, kudzu, fringed pink, bush clover, ague, and balloon flowers we had planted. Everything grew like crazy, despite the fact that there were more bugs than ever. The ban on Malathion had just gone into effect. My mother kept a fly swatter and box of tissues in every room of the house. The swatters all had extra-long handles. One night while we were in the living room with Ojiichan watching Japanese TV, broadcasted from San Francisco, a spider dropped down from the ceiling and rested smack in the center of the screen.

Ojiichan had a juice jar and paper ready, but my mother was quicker: She hated all bugs and insects, even those that were friends of nature. Driving all over town sharing that year's harvest, she almost wrecked the car half a dozen times. She rear-ended one guy and paid the damages out of pocket so that the insurance wouldn't go up. No matter how carefully she washed the vegetables or shook out the flowers, little riders remained. She would let out a shriek and stomp on the brakes while the silver-bug or aphid scurried up her arm and traffic behind us screeched and honked.

I started a new school that fall, where two of the Swan Girls attended grades ahead of me. In gym, I learned I could do three pull-ups. Social studies was my best subject, French and math my worst. At the time, the library was well-funded and therefore well-stocked, to my pleasure and benefit.

"Put that book down, get off that bag of fertilizer, help me out, here."

My mother lugged the potted palms over to the pool, where they were easily reached with the poolside hose. Other hoses snaked around the yard, irrigating where my mother's zealous planting exceeded even the reach of the monolithic automatic drip system that had been installed the year before.

"I really would like to be the Incredible Hulk," I said wistfully, holding the hose.

"What? Oh, Halloween, again?" She squinted. "What day is today, September thirtieth? Plenty of time. Wil, pay attention!"

I kept the palm from toppling into the pool. "I want to be something good this year." She had already informed me it would be my last Halloween. I was getting old for that kind of thing.

"No boys will like you if you're more of a boy than they are," my mother said, taking the hose from me. "Here, get it closer to this side."

"It's my last Halloween. I don't want to waste it in a dumb tutu."

"Watch your mouth. Grandma had her silk kimonos." She shook the hose out. I stepped over it. "You could be a Japanese lady."

"I don't see why I have to be what a boy's going to like," I said.

"You know what happens when you talk to your mother that way," my mother returned, catching my expression. She smacked her hands together. The hose jerked. "Ha! Flat as a frog."

According to my mother, there was once a girl who was always contrary. When the mother suggested she go to the mountains, the girl went to the sea. When the mother said she craved fish for dinner, the girl craved chicken.

Then the mother got sick and was on her deathbed. Thinking to outwit the girl, she said, "Please bury me by the riverbank.'' She actually wanted to be buried in the fields, but thought her daughter would act in the opposite way as usual.

The girl, however, honored the mother's wishes, and buried her beside the river, which flooded the next year and washed the mother's grave away. The girl, so contrary and disobedient, was crushed flat beneath a falling rock. My mother often pointed her out to me, a flat stone frog that had once been a disobedient daughter. Actually, Oji-ichan found the rock shaped like a frog in the Sierra Mountains, and brought it home to showcase in the garden, whereupon my grandmother provided the story for it.

''Turn on the tap,'' my mother ordered presently, bringing me back to the poolside, with the palms and the hot sun. Having just recently moved to California, sometimes I was surprised by my surroundings. Living at the ranch was different from visiting it, and I wasn't sure I liked it as well. Having family around all the time was a drag.

''Wil,'' my mother said, after I turned on the tap, ''Faith told Auntie she saw you in the quad at lunchtime, on the grass with your legs wide open.''

''I probably had a book between them, reading like this.'' I tried to demonstrate, standing. ''Faith's just like her mother,'' I said. ''A real snoop.''

My mother's lips thinned as she blasted the palms with her new power nozzle from Gotanda Hardware. ''Anyway,'' she said, raising her voice above the spray of water, ''nice girls don't do that kind of thing, and you know it.''

''But boys like it,'' I said, just to inflame her.

She turned the hose on me, and I shrieked at the

explosion of icy needles on my skin. Then she hit me with the hose, once. I could feel the bruise immediately.

"Your grandmother, so ashamed, if she heard you talking like that," my mother sniffed, giving the hose a yank. "Shame on you." She went to turn off the tap. "Here, help me carry these back, then you go inside. Shame on you."

It would have ended there, if my shoulder weren't bleeding where the hose struck, if she weren't so sure I would help her carry the palms around to the veranda without protest. Even if I had been given more of a choice than between being a ballerina or a geisha, I might have desisted. As it was, I dropped to the ground and rolled on my back, my skirt falling away as I kicked my legs. The sun was white light burning me down, sparking fireworks behind my open eyes. I thought of the phrase "dog days of summer," when ice on hot skin hissed and turned to steam, air conditioning was no match for nature, and people went crazy and out of control in an instant.

"I can do what I want!" I screamed.

She came toward me. I got confused, and rolled the wrong way, into the pool. I tried to surface, but her hands were on my head, holding me underwater. I heard her yelling at me, but then she started screaming.

A spider had dropped down the back of her shirt, to the waistband of her skirt. While she tore her shirt out of the waistband, shrieking like a firebell, Ojiichan came out of the house to see what was going on. I climbed out of the pool and collapsed. The sky appeared to be all heat and ash, burning white. I looked for a sign of observation and assistance, hoping that this was being recorded on a more cosmic level than my internal template and Oji-ichan's blurring memory, but it was all just empty, waiting sky.

My mother ran into the house, pushing past Ojiichan, and called Uncle Mas, who came immediately. They took me to the doctor. My mother told him I had tripped and fallen into the pool. Disinfectant was applied to my shoulder. My wet hair was wrapped in a towel to keep it from dripping all over the office. I was sent home with my mother, who didn't screech to a halt one single time and drove with the steering wheel so tight in her grip. She sat like that long after we had pulled safely into the drive at the ranch.

The next day, I passed out in class. I had a fever of 104.5. I was taken back to the doctor, who admitted me to Mercy Hospital. His father had been Ojiichan and my grandmother's doctor until he died, and now the son tended to all of us. He was Uncle Sen's age. They had been best friends in high school. It turned out that an abscess had formed in my ear; I had struggled so hard to breathe, I had burst a gland in my neck. The nurse was suspicious, and asked my mother a few questions in a sharp way my mother navigated with exacting politeness until the doctor intervened, telling the nurse I had always been the least graceful of all the girls.

If that fact had been marginally debatable before, it was cast in stone now. The burst gland destroyed my sense of balance, as sure as cutting the whiskers off a cat. For months, I couldn't bend over to pick up a pencil without falling over. When I walked, I lurched like a ship in high seas. After a few days of this, crutches were brought and fitted for me. I didn't need them in order to stand, but they did improve my gait, and my mother and everybody else seemed to appreciate the aesthetic adjustment.

All this damage did have one advantage: that Halloween, my last, I made a flawless Frankenstein. My knees were a mess from falling down. There was a four-inch scar down my neck, where the doctor had cut to remove the abscess. At Halloween, I still had the stitches, all fifty of them. At school, I won the most realistic costume in my grade. The prize was a certificate for dinner at a fancy steakhouse in town.

"You look great!" one of my teachers called to me as school let out for the day. I smiled happily, and waved my certificate. I was perfect.

Loss is only livable if it's put away properly, and at the ranch, the living aren't allowed life, and the dead never die. Every time my mother says something is "Mama's recipe," all I can taste is ash and bone. The highlight of this woman's social week is going to the mortuary. When my mother had the couches reupholstered, she had them covered in exactly the same material all over again.

My grandmother's funeral should have been closure and a farewell, but instead, it was meaningless pomp and pageantry. Afterward, Reverend Matsunaga led everyone outside the church and into the courtyard, and struck the gong as my grandmother's body was brought out of the temple. The gong was a great mossy thing beside the carp pond. Throwing pennies into the pond, the Swan Girls' and my coins glanced off the gong and sang with coppery resonance all the way down. We pulled at our tights and the hems of our new black dresses and talked about our wishes as symbolized by our pennies, now kissed by the fish.

Ojiichan stood on the temple steps, prayer beads ringing his hands. The sons, grandsons, and nephews of my grandparents' friends shut the hearse doors and stepped back from the curb. Lost white roses from the casketpiece were strewn upon the walkway, an inverted plain of stars beneath our feet. The Swan Girls and I plucked these blossoms and threw the petals over each other, a bittersweet echo of the Buddhist weddings we had attended or taken part in during our childhoods. We picked up the discarded roses and wove the stems into chains that we left at the altar in the temple. We all agreed that we had wanted to run after the hearse, but didn't know what we would have done had we been able to catch it.

The ranch never changes. At night, on the veranda, my mother's pots of succulents hang from the eves, in full bloom. The flowers are pink and purple, patterned irridescent. The silvery veins of my mother's hearts a'tangle shine in the moon's pale radiance. Luminous pink buds draw tight for the night, hen and chicks sleeping close together. One wee spider scampers down the side of the pot, vanishing into ashen shadows. Late summer fireflies light its way.

Senseless

~~~~~~~~~

The next day, on our way to visit Uncle Sen, my mother and I see that there's a funeral at the Buddhist church. My mother doesn't slow down as we drive past.

"You don't know the deceased?" I ask her, because there was once a time when she knew everybody, living and dead, connected with the church.

"They were *hakujin*."

That means white. My mother and I are dropping by Uncle Sen's house unannounced, an impropriety even in what are to my mother dire circumstances. The word *alcoholic* has probably never passed my mother's lips. Though the day is bright and the neighborhood tranquil, as we pull up to the house we see that the curtains are drawn, the darkened windows blinded eyes.

"We won't stay," my mother says.

"That's a relief," I say as she rings the bell. I slump against the entryway. "I hate coming home," I mutter.

"I don't see why," my mother says. "You need to relax."

"Well, that's the problem."

She turns the door knob, and peers inside the house. "Anybody here? Hello!"

"Let's go," I prod her.

At the same time that Aunt Ann emerges from the kitchen wiping her hands on a dishtowel, Uncle Sen staggers out from the hall that leads to the bedrooms. Over my mother's shoulder, I see that he's naked. Yet even this pales in interest to the gun he has in his hand, pointed at us. Immune to conventional sentiment, my mother pushes the door open and steps inside. Aunt Ann turns toward Uncle Sen, and in a remarkably courteous voice, asks him if he needs anything. Apparently, she's used to being held up at gunpoint in her own house, by her own husband.

He tells her to shut up. "Get out of here, Ava," he adds, waving the gun at my mother for the most effective punctuation I've ever seen.

I'm persuaded, but my mother isn't. "Put that gun down," she says.

Aunt Ann keeps the house spotless, and Uncle Sen is filthy. He smells like advanced disintegration. Save the purple patches under his eyes and a gouge on his head from a recent fall, he has no color. His flesh is so tender it bleeds at his touch, hence his lack of attire. When he scratches, he digs into itchy-looking patches on his chest and belly with the muzzle of his gun.

"Put that down," my mother repeats. "You're going to shoot one of us by mistake."

"Good," he says, and fires the gun into the ceiling. I hit the floor.

"Sen!" Aunt Ann screams, and he fires it again. Daylight and plaster flake down on our heads. "Stop it!"

I look up and see other holes in the ceiling. He might have shot those when Uncle Mas came to visit, but surely Uncle Mas would have mentioned it.

"It wouldn't be a mistake," Uncle Sen snarls.

Both breathing heavily, he and my mother stare at each other for a minute, then my mother turns to Aunt Ann. "You let him drink this way?" she demands incredulously. "How did he get like this?"

I almost groan aloud at this textbook codependency. "Come on, Mom," I say. "Let's go home."

"Get out of here, Ava," Uncle Sen says. "Go home."

He tosses the gun down, and I jump, thinking it's going to go off. Uncle Sen gives me a look, like, What's wrong with you? "Gee, I think I'll go wait in the car," I croak with what's left of my voice, and start to creep away.

My mother collars me. "You wait right here," she says. "Don't be such a baby."

"Get out of here!" Uncle Sen screams. "What's wrong with you? I have a gun," he warns us.

"Sen," my mother begins.

"If you won't leave," he says, "then I will."

Uncle Sen takes off toward the back of the house, grabbing his keys from the key rack as he goes. We hear the electric garage door going up.

"He can't drive," Aunt Ann whispers, "he's naked!"

I seize another set of keys off the rack, in case we have to follow him. We hurry outside, around to the garage. Two of the doors are open. We can see the old Wagoneer Aunt Ann uses for running errands around town. Uncle Sen and Aunt Ann have two Wagoneers and a Cherokee that's constantly in the shop.

Behind the other open garage door, Uncle Sen sits in the Cherokee, fumbling with his huge ring of keys. Aunt Ann goes to bang on the side of the car, then on the window. Uncle Sen slaps the locks down, and continues to peer at his keys. My mother looks around, agitated, as though someone from her gardening club might witness this. The neighborhood is quiet, except for the muffled sound of Uncle Sen cursing while he tries to figure out which key is which.

Exasperated, I tell my mother, "Call an ambulance."

"That would be a lot of trouble," my mother says vaguely.

"Look around you," I suggest.

"Sen," Aunt Ann yells.

"Call the police," I holler at her.

"Don't call the police," Aunt Ann screams, continuing to pound on the window. If anything, she's scaring Uncle Sen, who drops the keys on the floor.

I look at the keys in my hand. "Which is the one to that car there?" I ask, meaning the one Uncle Sen isn't in.

"How would I know?" My mother takes a step toward the garage. Uncle Sen is fishing for the keys under the seat. He finds them, fans them out, and begins jamming them one by one into the ignition. The last one fits and turns, and the engine coughs.

"Sen!" Aunt Ann screeches.

I race to the other car, Aunt Ann's Wagoneer, vault into the driver's seat, and start it up. I back it out so fast and at such a hard angle that part of the garage door frame splinters and flies off toward the road, but the Wagoneer is squarely behind Uncle Sen. If he wants to get out of the garage, he has to find a way to drive over the car that's now blocking his path.

Uncle Sen is honking and screaming. Aunt Ann is hitting the roof of the car with a broom *bong! bong! bong!* I throw the Wagoneer in reverse, back up, and reposition the car closer to the garage. In my haste, another length of wood is scraped off the door frame.

"Wil! Ava!" Aunt Ann screams, brandishing the broom. "Stop her!"

"What are you talking about? Stop *him*," my mother retorts, seeing Uncle Sen throw the car door open and stagger out. Aunt Ann almost falls down backing away from him, but he trips over the broom she's dropped, falls forward, catches himself on the side of the Cherokee, then trips again on the broom. He hits the concrete with such a thud, I'm sure he must be dead. I hurry around the car to see, but he's still breathing.

Hearing the gunshots, the neighbors had called the police. Later, we follow the ambulance in my mother's car. "Good thing you didn't have the keys to this car," my mother jokes, turning up the air conditioner. "Maybe you block Uncle Sen, he hits you, everybody's insurance premiums go sky high."

My hands still shake so much, I can't even smooth my hair. "Never," I tell my mother, shivering, "never ask me again why I don't like to come home, okay? I mean it. Just don't even ask." Driving past the church again, the mourners are filing out.

"Nobody we know," my mother murmurs. Neither of us speak the rest of the way to the hospital.

By the time he gets to the hospital, Uncle Sen doesn't have the faintest idea where he is or who's doing what to him. Before a nurse draws the curtain closed, I unblinkingly watch the medics insert a catheter. Like many who rise above early enslavement to poverty, pride is Uncle Sen's master. He and the rest of the world think he's his own boss, but they would be wrong. It's interesting to watch Uncle Sen be passively humiliated; if it were someone I respected, I would look away. In his temporary room, he comes to for a few seconds.

He spots my mother. "Bet you think you're right, now," are the first words out of his mouth.

"You rest," my mother says. But he's gone again.

Now, Aunt Ann and my mother are arguing about Uncle Sen. Aunt Ann holds my mother accountable for bringing Uncle Sen to a disastrous end, meaning the hospital. "He'll be so mad," Aunt Ann mourns.

"Let him be mad," my mother says.

"Like he isn't already," I add.

"He'll hate you," Aunt Ann says, trembling.

"Let him hate me," my mother says.

"He never had far to go to begin with," I chime in, so peevish I'm almost enjoying myself by now.

"But he'll hate me!" Aunt Ann begins to weep. "What will he think? You know he'll say I let this happen."

I don't understand how Aunt Ann can be so devoted to the man who once saw a well-appointed woman on the street and snarled, "Look at her! If she didn't have a pussy, she'd starve." Uncle Sen and Aunt Ann are like this: They and my parents were invited to a big dinner party. I was home for the weekend and went along. My parents and I arrived first. We were seated at one of three long tables seating twelve. Uncle Sen and Aunt Ann were the only couple at the table not there yet. The party was being hosted by a vice-president at Sumitomo Bank, the son of a friend of Ojiichan's. My parents knew everyone there except for two women at the end of the table, later introduced as mid-level execs at the bank.

The Math told a joke about penguins and armadillos and while people were still laughing at the punchline, Uncle Sen and Aunt Ann came in. The Math waved. Uncle Sen, instead of seating Aunt Ann or greeting his friends and relatives, spied the two women at the end of the table and said, "Hey, lookit that, I been missing something here." He shucked off his coat, handed it to a startled Aunt Ann, and motored on down without looking back.

"Sorry we're late," Aunt Ann apologized. "Sen drove."

That could have meant anything, from a detour over someone's lawn and dog, to a citation for speeding. During one trip from LA to San Francisco, Uncle Sen got two tickets. He should have been hauled to the hoosegow for a DUI both times, but wasn't.

The Math took Uncle Sen and Aunt Ann's coats to the coat check, got Aunt Ann a spritzer, and gave Uncle Sen a hard nudge on his way back from the bar. Uncle Sen went right on talking to those two women. The Math called between clenched teeth, "Sen! You're sitting up here, with us," and finally Uncle Sen boogied back to his place at the head of the table, slapped the Math on the back, and motioned for a drink.

"Sen," my mother said by way of chill greeting.

"Ava. Hey, I've got a great one," he announced to one and all. "You guys heard this joke yet?" He proceeded to trot out the same penguins and armadillos that the Math had unleashed a scant few minutes earlier.

I couldn't believe nobody told him they had just heard the joke. Worse, when one of the bank vice-presidents at our table told Aunt Ann she was lucky to be married to such a brilliant man, she agreed with him. The subject of this exchange would have agreed with them both, but he was down at the other end of the table again, getting those women's phone numbers. "Just let him be," I heard the Math tell my mother when she made a comment. Meanwhile, Aunt Ann was telling the bank guy that she didn't know what she would have done without Uncle Sen. "Be happy" came to my mind, but that was my own perspective. Aunt Ann seemed happy enough to bask in Uncle Sen's purported brilliance. She even brought his coat to him at the end of the evening, allowing herself to be introduced to the two women Uncle Sen had talked to all night. Everyone was smiling. I didn't get it.

But the evening did show me that so many people

have helped Uncle Sen be the way he is, he doesn't have a chance. During dinner, he was seated in the center and all of us radiated out from him. The configuration of the placement was that of a bullseye, concentric rings of fools with Uncle Sen in the middle, the biggest fool of all.

The Math arrives at the hospital, looking harried and uncomfortable. He glances at Uncle Sen, who's still out, and takes my mother and Aunt Ann into the hall. Thirstier than the hospital's tiny wax cups allow for, I toss my magazine aside and leave the room. In the hall, I ease past the Math, Aunt Ann, and my mother, who is talking fast. The faster a person talks, the better their short term memory works, the easier they retain and recall information, hence the smarter they are. My mother talks so fast, sometimes I can barely understand her. Which probably says something about me.

I find a soda machine in the basement cafeteria and occupy a hard yellow chair. After a minute, I get up again to get some candy. One of the ex's close friends comes in with a woman in tow. I want to dive beneath a table, but I just scrunch down small in a chair instead. They go straight to the pay phone and don't see me. At first, I think the ex has been in a motorcycle accident, the damage to his brain is massive, he doesn't have long to live. Maybe his friend is calling my number. The ex must have scratched out my name in his own blood at the scene. Maybe I have brain damage.

I remember that the friend's mother has kidney problems and he drives her to dialysis sometimes. The family lives near PCU. The father works in San Jose. The mother assists at the church when she's not sick. The ex's friend is okay. He wants to be a judge or a rock star. He's

reasonably disciplined, plays bass guitar, is not the bright-
est thing I've ever met, but as far as the legal system
and the airwaves go, I doubt that will be a factor. When
we first met, he was the ex's neighbor in the dorms.
He told me he had been trying to define the big diff
between a square and a well-rounded meal. He said he
was mulling it over without conclusion. He, the ex, and
I chewed on that one for several random nights. While
we were together, the ex and I didn't just waltz around
in semantics hell with each other, we danced with all our
friends, too.

The ex's friend spots me, hesitates, and shambles
over. The ex used to say the guy had the coordination
of a train wreck, but I like how he moves, with an un-
wieldy grace and lack of symmetry, like a damaged rocking
chair.

"Wil," he says. We survey each other. I lean to slap
him high five. He laughs. He's wearing a peace symbol on
a rawhide cord that's tarnished from him rubbing it constantly. It goes well with his "Eskimo Power" T and jeans
so tattered they look like they're about to spontaneously
decompose. His friend looks exactly like him, but not
quite so well groomed.

"You look fit," I tell him. He blushes and the friend
glares. She must be a girlfriend. "What happened to
what's-her-teeth?" I ask, meaning this guy's last victim of
love.

"Oh man, she went psycho."

"Yeah, I hate it when that happens."

"Me too. 'Til yesterday I was cleaning fish in Alaska.
Big reality check for me."

"I bet. What are you doing here?"

"Drove my mom." He hesitates. "You?"

"My uncle is here."

"Oh!" His brow clears. For some reason, he looks almost relieved. "Something serious?"

"No. Emergency reality check. He'll be fine."

"Good!" he exclaims. I smooth my hair and smile uncomprehendingly. Sez I, Lith and let lith. "I hear you're living at Pete Schrader's place down at the beach, and it's really nice," he goes on.

"It is. I imagine that violates your finely tuned proletariat sensibilities."

He seems to think I'm kidding about his sensibilities. "You look great, Wil," he says seriously. "When I first saw you a second ago, I thought you were a patient here."

Failing all footholds in the avalanche of my dignity, I finally ask, "He told you about the other hospital?"

"Other hospital? What do you mean? Oh," he says, getting it, "I get it. Yeah, I heard about that. What a bummer."

Lithium tempers instability and mood swings, but it does nothing for poor impulse control. I stand so suddenly, a flurry of M&Ms ricochet around us, and people turn to stare. "A bummer!" I repeat. "Naw, it was great. It was the biggest reality check of my life." I stomp off, not bothering with any further farewells. I almost bruise the tip of my index finger punching the elevator's "up" button.

The ex was untrustworthy and I gave him the perfect way to vindicate himself. He's right and I'm crazy. I hate it when I ask guys I know, "So, what happened to your girlfriend?" and they say, "She went psycho." I probably hate that because in the case of the ex and me, it's totally true.

Maybe I am going psycho. Maybe I'm there. I'm thinking about square versus rounded meals, that a square meal is filling but not necessarily healthful whereas the phrase *well-rounded meal* implies that certain nutritional requirements are satisfied.

I get off on the wrong floor and wind up alone in front of the nursery. The women in my family agree that there's freedom in losing a first love. After that, the only time a woman hurts that way again is after she has children. The Japanese familial unit is based on the relationship between mother and child, the Western model on a man and a woman. No one hurts anyone the way a first love does, or the way children do. First loves and children break every heart. The main difference between the two seems to be that in time, the former becomes slightly ridiculous, and sorrow over the latter only deepens and diffuses.

Square versus well-rounded meals! Where else but at college do people have the leisure to think about these things? I've heard or read that college years are the best years of your life. Later, will I miss what I'm not enjoying while it's happening? Did I really enjoy the ex while I had him? Now it seems like we were too busy fighting each other for our respective definitions of freedom to enjoy each other. The ex used to ask me, brown and green pondlike eyes luminous with unshed tears and aggrieved yearning, why he burns every bridge he ever builds. My eyes, heart, and everything else used to brim at that, but now I think his pyro tendencies have more to do with him shouting at me that I robbed him of his emotional freedom, when the opposite was true: The way we were together required that we had some.

When I realize that, I see him, really see him, for the first time in a long time, possibly ever. He looms in my rearview mirror, in my history, with a flamethrower.

Timepieces

〜〜〜〜〜〜

I'm running along a steep and rocky riverbank, and the earth is crumbling away beneath my feet until I'm splashing in the water, my feet stuck in the mud. The water is brown, and stinks of industrial waste and stagnation. My reflection in this water appears to have a depthless black face. I'm always about twelve years old in my dreams, slip-skinny with long white hair and large red eyes. Like a snake over my shoulder, a lightpost behind me arcs its neck toward the water to see this girl's image refracted through a dark prism of swamp.

"What does this mean?" the doctor asks, putting his pen down.

"I hope it doesn't mean I need more medication," I say weakly.

"Is that what your dream is telling us? I don't think so," the doctor says. "What does it signify to you?"

After the hospital, I started coming to Mercy Psych Center to have my lithium level checked on the fourth floor and my dreams deconstructed on the fifth. "I don't know," I say, and venture, "Fear of snakes?"

"Use your imagination," the doctor encourages me.

"I'd hate to have to swim in that river," I grimace.

He ignores me. "Does the river remind you of anything? Have you been thirsty lately?"

"If I wouldn't swim in it, I wouldn't drink it, either."

"Lithium is a salt," the doctor advises. "Make sure you stay hydrated."

"I don't know what I'm supposed to say," I admit at last.

"Do you feel self-conscious?"

"As opposed to self-aware?"

He picks up his pen. "Define the difference for me."

I hesitate. "It's the same big diff as that which exists between survival and life?"

"Try to stop being so literal. Tell me what the river reminds you of," the doctor prompts again.

Completely baffled now, I deliberately strive for the existential. "Nuclear war is survivable."

"Is this dream post-nuclear?"

"Maybe. Sort of. I never thought of it that way before." I form my sentences before I speak them. "My father's grandmother was in the 1945 bombing of Hiroshima. She saw the eye of the blast open over the city."

"Go on," he nods.

I sit up. "I remember being told that by the river, crawling with people, metal lampposts bent their necks to the water. My father's grandmother joined the exile of people leaving the city. Some girl confused her for her mother, and my father's grandmother had to kick her away. She died when I was three, but in photographs, she has no hair. After the bomb, her scalp slipped off her skull like a cap. She survived because of her clothing. She was wearing a white kimono, for her husband, who had died in the navy. She was in the Buddhist Forty-Nine Days of Mourning. She thought the girl who mistook her for some-one else might have been the daughter of a dead navy man: There were thousands of women wearing white kimonos by the end of the war."

The doctor squints at me. "You describe the reflec-tion in the water as being dark-skinned, white-haired, red-eyed," he says, referring to his notes. "Does it occur to you that this reflection is your photographic opposite?"

"What do you mean?"

"What you've described as your reflection is actually a mental negative of yourself," the doctor tells me. "I'd like to propose that it's an alter-ego snapshot, trapped underwater in this awful river. So," he expands, crossing his legs, "tell me more about the river."

I shrug. "I don't even own a camera."

Holding a cotton ball to the crook of my arm after my blood work, I step off the elevator and run right into my cousin Hope, the family black sheep. "Mina," she gasps, and looking at her, for a moment, I forget who I am. "Mina, you look great."

"That has to be a sign of something terribly wrong in your life," I tell her, "when everybody says how great you look."

"Oh! But you do. Mina," she says, "I'm pregnant."

"You are," I affirm witlessly, noting what I had just marked down as increased girth. She seems happy. "That's great."

"It's a girl," she says.

"Congratulations. Do you have a name picked out?"

"Not yet." She laughs. "Is *What to Name the Baby* still at the ranch?"

"Nothing ever changes at the ranch."

"Do you have time to wait for me?" Hope asks. "I have an appointment now, but I'll be done in fifty minutes. We could walk over to my place afterward, it's about five blocks from here."

I follow Hope back up to the fourth floor and linger in the lobby during her fifty-minute hour. She comes out promptly at ten to five, saying, "I started coming here when I found out I was pregnant. It's expensive, but worth it."

"You think?"

"Sure." She lowers her voice in the elevator. "I wanted to make sure I had my head on straight before I had a baby to take care of."

"That's great. That's unlike the family," I comment as we step out. "No one else ever bothered."

"Dad's all Zen, never questions anything," she agrees. "Why ask why?"

"No, Zen is, Why ask why ask why?" I hold the door for her. "Your dad just has terminal lockjaw." I expect her to ask after him, but she doesn't, and we head up the street together.

The place she shares with Avery is a Victorian walk-up. From the sidewalk, I see amps and speakers crowding the windows. Hope holds up her key ring for my inspection. "One key," she says, and when I don't get it, she elaborates. "I feel sorry for people with more than five keys. I have my home, and no doors to unlock other than this one."

"Freedom of choice is freedom from choice," I parrot.

"I never thought of it that way before," Hope says, and laughs.

Once inside, a shopping cart full of parcels of every shape and dimension sits in the hallway. Envelopes are bundled in the cart seat, sectioned with rubber bands. "What are these?" I ask as we squeeze by. I start to take off my shoes, glance at the floor, and decide to leave them on. I'm wearing brand new socks.

"One of Avery's friends is a mail carrier," Hope explains, putting her purse and key down on the desk that competes for space with a dirty green sofa and three folding chairs, two with a board across them. A goldfish bowl and plants in brightly painted pots balance atop the make-shift table. A dusty Matisse print hangs over the couch. "Sometimes we take over part of his route for extra money."

"Is that legal?"

"Helping a friend out? Why not?"

It sounds like a felony to me, but that's not a sociable thing to say. I wish Hope would offer me something to drink, but instead, she sits on the free folding chair, sighing, "It's already hard for me to get up from the couch, once I sit down."

The certainty that coming here was a giant mistake grips me suddenly, and I have to pry my tongue off the roof of my mouth. "How far along are you?" I manage.

"Five months," she says, rubbing her back. "It's amazing."

I look around the apartment. The kitchen, bedroom, and what I assume is the door to the bathroom are all visible from my low vantage point on the couch. Crumpled Marlboro packs, a tote erupting dirty laundry, and stacks of neon fliers promoting a benefit gig at Bottom of the Hill spill in a puddle by the music equipment. A Danielle Steel paperback straddles two frames resting behind the fishbowl and propped up against the metal backrest of the folding chairs. The first frame contains Avery's college diploma behind cracked glass. The fishbowl magnifies the cracks, and Avery's full name. Wreckage of what once were two canebrake chairs has been fused together to form a coat rack upon which rain garments drape practically in my face. The empty round O of the seat holds umbrellas and croquet mallets. Beyond the living room, the kitchen is so small that if Hope dropped something on the floor, she'd have to kick it out to the living room to pick it up. The bed is obscured beneath either a poster or a sheet of wrapping paper. It appears to be bursting out of the bedroom doorway. Yet despite the mess, there's an impersonal air to this place, as though it's only temporary. I wonder where the baby's going to sleep—in the oven?

"We'll put the baby in the tub until we find a

bigger place," Hope lets me know, following my eyes.

"There's a fancy French bassinette at the ranch," I say. "I saw it just the other day. It seats three," I add superfluously.

"Sometimes I see Faith," Hope says at last.

I nod. "She told me."

Hope flares at that. "That's one thing I always hated about the family," she says. "Information as power. It gives people such a sense of self-importance to bear bad news."

"Gee," I say. "Relax."

"What else did Faith tell you? You know," she goes on before I can answer, "you don't have to have tons of money and a bourgeois husband and lifestyle to have a baby."

"Are you planning to marry Avery?" I ask.

"I knew you'd ask that," she says, sounding triumphant that I've done no better than she expected of me. "We aren't planning on it, no."

"That'll be difficult," slips out of my mouth. I continue with reluctance. "Not having family, I mean."

"God," she says. "You're so hung up on the idea of family, like it ever turns out the way you hope it will. Family just ruins your life."

Fighting the uncharacteristic urge to defend the idea of family, I say, "The best way to avoid disappointment is to avoid desire," thinking she'll flare again.

"Exactly," she agrees instead. "What time is it?"

I flash my bare wrist. "I don't have a watch."

"I don't have one, either," Hope says. "I have to take Avery dinner down at the club at six-thirty."

"I should go," I murmur.

"You could come along," she says. "Avery's opening for Aviary, six English girls with guitars."

"I'm not twenty-one yet." I count on my fingers. "Six days."

"No fake ID?"

"No. I don't drink alcohol anyway. Hope, would you like me to ask after the bassinette? Joy always wants everything new, and nobody else is close to having children yet."

Hope studies me. "No boyfriend?"

"No one whose children I'd want to have. Faith set me up on a blind date," I remember. "That's the day after tomorrow. I'll get back to you next week."

"Is he a nice Japanese boy?" Hope smirks, making me depressed for this man whom I've never met and had previously vowed to loathe. "Good marriage material?"

No Honky Inferno, I want to say but instead reiterate, "I'd better go now." As we get around the shopping cart on our way out, I look at the top package. "Shouldn't these be delivered today?" I ask, thinking, Federal offense!

"Oh, I have to do that before I leave," Hope says. "I almost forgot."

The desk's top drawer holds two big rings of postal keys. Turns out, Avery and Hope occasionally tackle segments of two different routes. When I leave, Hope has turned on the desk lamp and is sorting through the drawer's contents, hunched over her treasure trove of mailbox keys. I stare a moment, but Hope doesn't appear to notice.

"I'll see about the bassinette," I say finally.

"Whatever," she says, not looking up.

"Do you want me to help you before I go?" I ask.

"That's okay," she says. "I know dinner's at seven-thirty every night at the ranch."

I touch the doorknob. "Hope," I say, and she looks at me. "You should come by sometime."

"Why?" she asks.

"Just what would happen if, for some reason, you no longer had Avery?"

"I'd have no one. God! What's wrong with you? That's a macabre question, at twenty," she says.

Her answer strikes me the far more macabre. "I'll call about the bassinette," I mumble. Glancing around for the last time, I plan to rustle up a clock, too, and maybe a mirror. Clutter aside, this apartment seems like a space in which the inhabitants have no sense of life's measure, nor any sense of self. Instead of a place where two occupants share a life, this apartment feels like a dusty shell wherein two people are failing to understand the passage of time.

Hope goes back to her keys. "Thanks for stopping by," she says.

Sticks and Stones

~~~~~~~~

The day after I see Hope at the hospital, Uncle Mas is sitting on the veranda, smoking. My mother strives to monitor his diet and occasionally campaigns to shame him into going to the doctor, but she doesn't comment on his cigarettes. She heard somewhere it takes seven seconds for nicotine to reach the smoker's brain, and she says far be it from her to rob Uncle Mas of the only comfort he has that's so accessible it takes only seven seconds to obtain. Her only request is that he not smoke in the kitchen during meals. We pull into the drive, he waits for us to get out of the car, and follows us into the house.

"Want something to drink?" I ask him, waving a can of soda his direction.

"Not soda."

Continuing our conversation from the car as though there was no interruption, my mother heads straight for her "Things to Do" board, and draws: 晶. " '日' is sun," she says, pointing. " '晶' is shiny."

"I know that," I sulk, sitting at the table. In this way, I learned about five hundred Japanese characters. I learned that 木 means tree, and 森 means forest. 女 is woman, and 姦 is noisy.

She's mad. "Then why do you look blank when I say your hair looks pretty shiny?"

"Because you said 'shiny' in Japanese," I said, tossing the pop top. "I don't think fast in Japanese. I got a haircut," I explain to Uncle Mas.

"What's wrong, Masa?" my mother asks, capping the marker. "You go see Sen?"

"Yup." He takes one last drag on his cigarette and tosses it in the sink.

"Is he worse? They run those tests today?"

"AIDS," Uncle Mas says cryptically. Uncle Mas's siblings understand his one- and two-word declarations perfectly. For example, if Uncle Mas says, "Fish," apropos nothing, it could mean he saw one, ate one, caught one. But my mother will cross the room to change the channel to the PBS fishing show, if Uncles Sen or Wes haven't done so already. About half their comprehension is probably contextual, but otherwise, they seem to pluck his thought waves right out of thin air. It has nothing to do with time elapsed. Aunt Em has been with him for thirty years, and their relationship has been the textbook definition of miscommunication. Their children don't understand Uncle Mas at all. "Huh, Dad? What? What do you want?" It's a mystery.

"Sen has AIDS?" My mother jokes, rinsing and filling the kettle.

"Asked for test."

My mother marvels for a moment, then bangs the kettle down on the stove. "You see Ann there?" When Uncle Mas indicates negatively, she asks, "Well, where was she? She's the one who should be with him."

"Home."

"Those who worry about it the most are the least likely to get it," I observe.

"What are you talking about?" my mother asks, vexed.

"AIDS. But illness aside, that's true of practically everything."

My mother blinks. "Why should Sen worry at all?" she asks finally. She lingers over her cup of tea, takes off her earrings and stashes them back in Ojiichan's go table drawer with the rest of her good jewelry, and changes into her regular clothes. Uncle Mas drives us over to Uncle Sen's house, with the unspoken assumption that we'll go with Aunt Ann to the hospital for evening visiting hours.

Jennifer greets us at the door. Inside, we see that Aunt Ann has been baking. The whole house smells sickening-sweet, like a pastry shop. In the kitchen, the counters are covered with fruit tarts, pies, and deep-dish cobblers. Aunt Ann is the only person I know who makes double-scalloped crusts, so flaky and perfect they taste French. Her kitchen is huge and recently remodeled, all in creams and butter yellows. The sink is spotless, the drying rack full. The dishwasher is running. My mother fans herself, and Jennifer goes to turn the air conditioning up. It's hot from the sun, the yellow walls, and the oven. Uncle Mas inspects a platter of deep-dish apple cupcakes.

"Have one," Aunt Ann says, and together, we all crane toward the counter. "The apples are from the Shimizus' orchard."

"When did Jennifer come home?" my mother inquires.

"Just this morning," Aunt Ann says, handing Uncle Mas a napkin.

"We thought you would be at the hospital," my mother says, a lie but face-saving for everyone: My mother isn't put in the awkward position of confronting Aunt Ann about not being at the hospital, and of her own free will, Aunt Ann can tell my mother that she didn't go today.

"I didn't go today," she says, watching Uncle Mas dally among the tarts. "I've been busy at home."

My mother doesn't say anything. Jennifer doesn't return. Aunt Ann serves tea, then turns off the lights in the kitchen and leads us into the family room. The TV is on, tuned to a soap opera. Uncle Sen's deluxe entertainment center is undisturbed, the bar hidden from view, the books and rocks in their proper places. Ojiichan's rocks are beautiful, and immensely serene, timeless symbols of time. I know the names of each of them. Running my hand over their cool surfaces, this knowledge pleases me, and my pleasure takes me by surprise.

My mother smooths her skirt, and perches beside Aunt Ann. They were once like sisters; my mother admired Aunt Ann very much. My mother is eight years younger than Uncle Sen, six years younger than Aunt Ann.

When Uncle Sen and Aunt Ann were courting, Aunt Ann used to invite my mother along to the movies and soda shop.

Aunt Ann comes from a family of some substance. Despite the father's gambling problem, they were well-to-do. The only poverty they suffered was a dearth of sons. Aunt Ann was the youngest of seven daughters, all of whom married well. To this day, Aunt Ann and her sisters are pointed to by their elders and peers as paragons of model marriage. The Munemori girls, as they're known some thirty years after girlhood, are uniformly sheltered, snide, and snooty to varying degrees. My mother says they used to have a lot of fun together when they were young. Aunt Ann, her two sisters who still lived at home, and my mother would moon around listening to 78s Aunt Ann's father would bring home from the record store in the city. While their peers frequented dance halls and did the frug, the girls would do one another's nails, talk about the boys they liked, and listen to Bing Crosby for hours on end. "Careless hands," my mother sometimes sings as she does the dishes, "don't care when dreams slip through."

My mother was a bridesmaid at Aunt Ann's wedding. Years later, I borrowed her dress for my first dance, and kept it. The Swan Girls loved it. It's a cream silk sheath held together with clusters of seed pearls. My grandmother made it, beading the pearls by hand. It fell to my mother's ankles; I wore it at knee-length and my mother put a flower behind my ear that I threw away as soon as I got to the dance.

"I plan to take Jennifer to the hospital tonight," Aunt Ann says. "She hasn't seen Sen in so long. It seemed like Ashley and she were always at school after . . . after a certain point. Sen insisted they get the best education possible, but it didn't matter to me." She trails off. "Girls don't need fancy educations like boys do."

"Daughters you raise to serve others," my mother says with wintry certainty, "sons, for yourself." This strikes me as cruel in light of Aunt Ann's lack of both brothers and sons, but my mother gets to the point. "I hear Sen requested more tests."

"Oh, Ava." Aunt Ann glances at me. "Maybe we should talk about this later."

My mother sends me away. On my way out, I tour the front room and Uncle Sen's office. The front room is where Aunt Ann keeps her *kokeshi* dolls. The custom cases line the walls.

Kokeshi comes from *ko*, "child," and *keshi*, "erase." The first *kokeshi* dolls were carved to honor daughters that had been "erased." Their faces are all solemn, framed with black bangs and folds of multilayered kimonos that reach the throat. Some of Aunt Ann's dolls are valuable antiques, dating back to nineteenth-century, Meiji Japan, when rural families were forced to resort to infanticide, and *kokeshi* were routine. In order to survive, the family was *mabiki*, "weeded out," the same expression used for rice seedlings when some are sacrificed in order for those that remain to have space and nourishment to thrive.

Uncle Sen's office is off the *kokeshi* room. His desk is clean. He never attended college. Photographs, community awards, and an NRA plaque hang on the wall behind his desk instead of diplomas. On the wall facing his desk is his war memorabilia, that which he once pointed out to me as more important than the happy adornment on the opposite wall. "Japs!" each item proclaims loud and clear, while everything behind his desk is mute testimony to his life as a solid American. But when he sits at his desk, the future is behind him. When he established his office in what was once a sitting room off the foyer, he doomed himself to forever gazing at the past.

Outside, I trot down to the garage and inspect the structural damage I created the other day. Uncle Mas comes out of the house, and lights up a cigarette. He walks down to the garage, takes a look, then comes over to me.

"Are they done talking yet?"

He answers negatively, slumping against the garage door.

"Are you okay? You ate that tart," I diagnose.

"Two."

I shake my head. Aunt Ann's kitchen was like that of the witch in Hansel and Gretel. There was too much sweetness in the air, an aura of glaze and fury, the brittle memory of happiness from long ago that Aunt Ann was trying to encase in a pastry shell. All day long, she had been baking a lifetime of anger and denial into perfect pies with double-scalloped crusts.

"Don't smoke," I tell him. "You really should go to the doctor."

"What for?"

"A check-up."

"Gonna die anyway."

Uncle Mas lapses into his usual silence, and held hostage to his nonverbal social edict, I study him. Though I see him more than any other relative, he's the one whom I understand the least. His wordlessness aggravates my already minimalist comprehension where the family is concerned. While I could conceivably sift through Uncle Sen's lingual landslides if I chose to do so, and have grown adept at discerning my mother's real meanings and intentions from her word and deed, Uncle Mas is best compared to a made bed: I can only imagine what would be revealed if I were somehow able to pry the covers up.

"Well," I begin. Compared to Uncle Mas, I'm a magpie. "I ran into Hope yesterday."

"Where?"

I swallow. There's a definite hierarchy of acceptable debacle we all adhere to. Speeding violations, lax dental hygiene resulting in root canals and bridges, and attending a substandard university are activities frowned upon but not suppressed. In fact, they often become fodder for intergenerational hilarity as tire boots, astronomical dental bills, or a BA as opposed to a BS become jokes with a half-life that rivals plutonium.

Flunking a class or being fired from a job are discussed in hushed tones when the offending party is absent. Public transgressions are regarded as being potentially humiliating for the entire group, so except in the most radical cases, report of this kind of offense is accompanied by a declaration of remedial ambition: Mid-level failure is unfailingly appended with hope.

However, alcholism, cancer, and mental illness are the gravest of sins, not discussed at all if the perpetrator is family (although the reverse applies if the perp is not a family member; the ideal perp is a close friend of the family, preferably reclining back in mutual history three generations at a minimum). Uncle Mas knows every detail of my mother's daily activities, thoughts and opinions, joint tax return. "Don't tell him about the hospital," she warned me while I was still there. "He couldn't stand to know."

"Where?" Uncle Mas asks again.

"I don't know," I say finally. "I just happened to run into Hope." When he says nothing, I tell him, "I thought I'd send her some stuff from the ranch."

"If you want," he says.

"Have you ever thought about contacting her?"

"No."

"She's pregnant," I tell him, mindful of being the bearer of bad news, and also conscious that it feels kind of good, as Hope said.

"I know," Uncle Mas says.

He doesn't appear to be about to divulge more, so I change the subject. "Well, looks like Uncle Sen's been cheating on Aunt Ann," I hear myself say. What is there to talk about in this family? When Uncle Mas doesn't answer, I tell him, "You should have seen him, Uncle Mas. For everyday torture, it's hard to beat witnessing to someone else's self-abasement."

Uncle Mas grinds his cigarette out with his boot. "Grandma, too?"

My grandmother was deeply ashamed of her cancer. She had known she was going to die, and wished she would die faster. She requested that her doctor not tell anybody she was sick. She never asked for much, and her only wish on her death bed was to die without the pity of her friends. Toward the end, she was bone-thin, wig askew on her forehead, drinking Ensure instead of eating solid food.

I hesitate. "That was different."

"Same, sick." Uncle Mas looks at me. "Can't help."

I used to not like Uncle Mas very much. He bored me. He didn't play video games with me and joke around, the way Uncle Sen did. Uncle Mas never brings anything special to my mother the way Uncle Wes always does, showing up with See's candy, a flat of strawberries from Watsonville, fresh chicken. I always found Uncle Mas drab, a frog on a log. It requires no stretch of the imagination to picture his tongue popping out suddenly, catching a fly or a raindrop. But one day, my grandmother told me a story about Uncle Mas that changed the way I saw him for good.

When he was a boy, Uncle Mas cut school a lot. Ojiichan found out, and chased him with a saw. One time, he slammed Uncle Mas's head down on the kitchen table so hard, the table cracked. Before the war, he caught Uncle Mas stealing cigarettes from him, and made him burn himself with a lit cigarette on the back of his hand.

"He made Masa burn himself?" everybody wonders whenever these stories are told. Nobody thinks to term it child abuse, because that was simply Ojiichan. His view of suffering was a dual one. He believed everyone needed to suffer in order to be strong, but he also used to point out that in no other country except America is the ordinary citizen's right to happiness written in the national charter.

"Life, liberty, and the pursuit of happiness," Thomas Jefferson wrote, his bequest to every American citizen. Ojiichan loved The Declaration of Independence and the Constitution: Before he became a naturalized citizen, he carried a copy of the Constitution in his wallet and took it with him everywhere he went. He quoted from it freely. After Pearl Harbor, when federal agents came to Ojiichan and my grandmother's house to take him away, upon learning that they hadn't brought a search warrant, Ojiichan brought out his Constitution and cited the Fourth Amendment rights. Not his own, but those of his children, born in the United States, that "the right of the people to be secure in their persons, houses, papers and effects, against unreasonable searches and seizures shall not be violated, and no warrants shall issue, but upon probable cause, supported by oath or affirmation, and particularly describing the place to be searched, and the persons or things to be seized." They weren't interested in the American citizens in the household, however, and searched the house, arrested Ojiichan, and took him away, the Constitution neatly folded again and put back in his wallet.

"Didn't that make you mad?" I once asked Ojiichan.

He was surprised. "How they know?" he asked me, giving his cigarette an agitated swivel. "I a Jap," he said, pointing emphatically at his chest. "They right to search, right to question. Stupid, how you think we win war?"

Ojiichan and Uncle Mas were doomed from the start. At the end of Ojiichan's life, his temper would flare, and he would call for my mother, "*Oi!*," pounding on the armrests of his recliner, or sometimes groping around to see if anybody was there. Once, I saw Uncle Mas standing in the darkened dining room after dinner, watching his father reach out to shadows. I stood only a few feet away from both of them, but I wondered what Uncle Mas saw.

Ojiichan was a great go player. One of his friends ran a Pacific Rim import/export business, and gave Oji-

ichan an antique go table when Ojiichan retired. The table
was hand-carved, with hidden drawers that slid out of the
bottom for the stones. The stones were all onyx and ivory,
and my mother talked about making a necklace from a
handful of each. Instead, after Ojiichan died, the table was
used as a magazine rack, my mother put the stones in the
bottoms of crystal vases to prop flower stems and hid her
more valuable jewelry in the drawers.

Deemed a Japanese cultural item, the government
barred Ojiichan from taking his old go table with him into
camp, so he made one. Internees often turned to wood-
working and hand crafts to combat boredom. Ojiichan acquired wood from requisitions. The mountain area the
internment camp was built in was deliberately chosen for
its remoteness, but the mountains were rich in obsidian
and white quartz. This is when Ojiichan began to educate
himself about rocks. Obsidian was one of the hardest sub-
stances known to man, and was easily shaped down to a
thickness no greater than a molecule. Surgical instruments
could be made from obsidian. White quartz was less dis-
tinctive, but more beautiful if handled properly. White
quartz could be made to resemble moonstone, suffused
with a milky glow.

Kept behind barbed wire by armed guards in lookout
towers surrounding the camp, Ojiichan must have relied
on visitors from outside the camp to get his stones. Or
maybe he snuck out, over or under the fence, and walked
free at night. Some, usually rebellious young boys, did. In
any event, Ojiichan found a way to bring the mountains
to his barracks. He learned to shape and polish quartz
veined with orange borax, and obsidian black and bright,
with edges that cut metal and skin.

Uncle Mas was fascinated with the go board. He begged Ojiichan to let him play with it. Ojiichan told him not to go near the board, and one day in the mess hall, Ojiichan suddenly grabbed Uncle Mas's hand. Uncle Mas tried to pull away, but Ojiichan held tight.

"That's a deep cut you have on your finger, Masa," he observed, and let go.

Later, he brought down the go board and the stones, smooth quartz and biting obsidian, and asked my grandmother, "Where is he?"

He then set about teaching Uncle Mas how to play —not the five-in-a-row kind of go that children and Westerners play, but the real thing. Uncle Mas learned quickly. He had an aptitude for strategy: in the end, both too much so, and not enough. Ojiichan's friends would gather around, joke, give Uncle Mas hints, and make friendly wagers about how many moves it would take Ojiichan to win. The nightly face-off between Ojiichan and Uncle Mas became community entertainment.

Uncle Mas winning was never a question, but one day it happened. About six months after he started playing, he beat Ojiichan. And Ojiichan made him swallow one of his own stones.

This was Uncle Mas's victory, and his punishment. Uncle Mas thought Ojiichan was joking, but he wasn't. He insisted Uncle Mas swallow the stone. Uncle Mas reasoned that as the winner, he should choose whether or not he had to swallow the stone. Ojiichan said it was his "*tadai no gisei o haratte eta shyori*," his conquest, having exceeded his master, and his punishment for the same reason—the Japanese equivalent of Pyrrhic victory.

Uncle Mas swallowed the stone, and he stopped playing go. During the day, he avoided Ojiichan, which wasn't hard to do. Families disintegrated in the camps, as angry and alienated fathers out of work and frustrated mothers punished their children more and pushed them away. Children played with and ate meals with their friends.

Uncle Mas still returned to sleep every night, but after his big win, he made himself scarce. His cot was closest to the door, and every morning, he was the one who talked to the headcounter. The headcounter made the rounds every morning to confirm that no one had run off during the night. When the headcounter banged on the door, Uncle Mas was supposed to call out, "Six!" Sometimes he shouted out, "Ten!" and "A hundred!" and "Nobody!" But after his go win, he stopped being caustic, and started disappearing after the headcounter came and went. The next time my grandmother saw him was when she was called to the infirmary after Uncle Mas had been found in the latrine trying to pass a huge fecal boulder. He was rushed to the hospital and operated on. The doctor said he would be fine.

There were no fresh fruits and vegetables to speak of in camp. Most meals consisted of mutton and either rice or potatoes. The camp doctor assured Ojiichan and my grandmother that constipation was entirely normal in camp, but it seemed that there had been an inorganic stoppage of Uncle Mas's bowels: during his operation, the doctor extracted one perfectly round, flat, knife-edged obsidian stone.

"Remember that story about Uncle Mas?" I asked my mother one day. "The go stone Ojiichan made him swallow?"

"Nobody made anybody swallow anything," my mother said.

"Then why does Uncle Mas have a bad stomach?"

"Because he can't express himself."

"You mean, talk?"

When he was released from the camp infirmary, Uncle Mas was whole again, except that he stopped talking. My grandmother tried to coax him into talking with precious contraband nougat Ann Sayles had sent in a package of sweets. Ojiichan never said anything about why Uncle Mas had swallowed the stone, and from that point onward, Uncle Mas said almost nothing at all.

A week later, he suddenly slumped over. He was rushed back to the infirmary. There were lots of cuts in Uncle Mas's large intestine; they had ruptured and were bleeding. The doctor removed four feet of Uncle Mas's large intestine and sewed him up again.

"Don't you remember?" I prodded my mother. "Grandma told me."

"I was a baby then. Besides, sometimes she just liked to tell you stories."

But Uncle Mas still has terrible troubles with his stomach, and he still refuses to play go. I saw him studying Ojiichan's fancy table once. Uncle Mas ran his hand over the top, touched the carvings, and, pulling back in order to see, squinted at the inlaid grid. He opened the drawers and studied the stones. He held one of the smooth black onyx in his palm, rolling it back and forth. And then he walked away.

———

Uncle Mas finishes his cigarette, and we go back inside together. My mother and Aunt Ann are still in the living room, talking with their heads close together. Jennifer has joined them. They all three share the same posture, the same mannerisms. They don't see us. But on the table between them, on folded piece of black construction paper, something catches my eye and gleams like fool's gold: three perfect strands of long blond hair.

Sansei Inferno

E ven after the ex and I went our separate ways, I attended our Thursday-at-two therapy appointments alone. Altogether, I only saw this therapist half a dozen times, and felt slightly foolish returning to him once or twice without the catalyst of my decline in tow. But he already knew every detail of my misery, vanity, and pain, and I saw no reason to do anything by halves.

I found my abortion in the Yellow Pages. The only person with whom I shared this information was the therapist, whose name I no longer recall. I never saw him again after the appointment during which I divulged the source of my pregnancy termination information.

In a different setting, the restaurant where Jeff takes

me for dinner, I don't recognize the therapist until he touches my shoulder and says my name. "This is Jeff," I introduce my date, and pause.

"I'm Warren," the therapist supplies, glancing at me.

"Warren," I repeat as the two men shake hands. I had no idea what the therapist's first name was. "Warren," I marvel, "so how are you?"

When Jeff and I are seated at our table, he asks me, "Who was that?"

"My therapist," I answer.

"That's very vogue," Jeff nods, and opens his menu. A few minutes later, the waiter appears and Jeff orders, for me as well as himself: lobster bisque and lobster thermidor. I half-expected a lobster flambe for dessert, but it's crème brûlée instead.

The only way Jeff can express himself is through employment analogies. It's never clear to me exactly what he does, but he makes it obvious that he's central to the smooth operation of the firm. He actually calls it that—"the firm." My head hurts. The brûlée is smooth and sweet and good. Under the table, I wiggle my toes in their modified motorcycle boots, imagining how delicious it will be to have said boot planted on Faith's throat sometime soon. When Jeff picked me up, he said, "Nice boots." Taking into account his rep tie, navy blazer, and arch expression, it didn't take a genius to see he wasn't serious. "I thought Faith told you I'm much more about *personality*," I said, but he didn't get it.

The only thing we have in common is that we're

both third-generation Americans. Jeff gets himself another
drink. After he'd ordered our food, he let me know that
he has the enzyme that breaks down alcohol, but he lacks
the one that breaks down lactose in milk products. "I
forget what it's called," he said.

Name That Enzyme: I yawn. Jeff asks me what kind
of music I like, and I start to tell him. In a single but-
enough-about-you gesture, he turns the conversation
around to the latest club rage, a band called Honky Inferno. He has tickets to go see them tonight. Though I
beg exhaustion, curfew, and a death in the family, we wind
up at a sweaty little dance burrow, where he tries to
convince me to have a drink.

When I decline for the fifth time that evening,
he lets me know, "I think I've met your attitude before." I couldn't care less even as he begrudges me my
ginger ale. In my imagination, my boot isn't on Faith's
throat anymore but on her face. I am furious at being
fodder for this boor, and when Jeff stands and asks
me to dance, I throw myself into the bass groove with
such abandon, he watches me with renewed interest. I
bump my booty around the floor so that Jeff has no
choice but to follow. He can't be hungry after Hoovering
down all that lobster at dinner, what remained on my plate
as well as his own, but he's looking at me like I'm a
snack.

Hope is standing off to one side of the stage, and
although there must be at least two hundred people dancing under uncertain light, she is fixed on me. She's laughing at me. I see this despite the strobe lights, the other
bodies crashing into mine, the sweat and tears in my eyes.

When the music resumes after a set break, Avery, on stage, introduces Hope to the audience. She beams, and surprises me back into myself by curtsying the way she used to do in the living room at the ranch, after performing to Tchaikovsky with her sisters.

As the crowd applauds and Hope recedes into crunchy guitar licks and her own glow, I stop. Jeff bumps into me. I wonder if the Swan Girls and I were raised in such a loveless environment that we have grown up to be women who go out into the larger world desperate to prove ourselves worthy of love. It's obvious where it came from. Aunt Em indulges Uncle Mas in his ecliptic silences. Aunt Ann sorts through Uncle Sen's laundry, and over the course of five years saves three strands of blond hair she finds on his shirts. My mother alters her desires to accommodate the Math, the uncles, Ojiichan before he died. Standing before me, Hope looks as though she could survive on Avery's recognition for a lifetime.

I suddenly despise dating, the Swan Girls, family in general, all of humankind. Maybe I'll feel better in the morning, but I doubt it. Jeff is indicating I should kiss him. I reject this outright. Obvious resistance to this idea aside, I know that in this frame of mind, I'd probably turn into a toad.

By far, the worst date I ever had was with the ex. Early on, we went to a protest at city hall. Protestors swarmed the nearby freeway, shutting it down. The police were on edge, anticipating another shutdown. There were two guys with bullhorns. No beer, no bands. I don't remember what the protest was for. The bullhorn bozos seemed to

be yelling mostly at each other, although the more ob-
noxious of the two kept trying to mobilize everybody, as
though at a rock concert. There was no cohesive plan,
unless everybody wearing comfortable shoes and bringing
along a bottle of Evian could be called authoritative fore-
sight for the revolution.

"This is silly," I told the ex.

All of a sudden, there was the sound of sirens getting
closer. The police that were monitoring us told us to get
behind the monument. There was a statue in front of city
hall, a founding father bearing the graffitied legend, "Dead
White Male." We crowded behind him. Cars were approaching, screeching around corners, sirens growing
louder.

Shots rang out. Everybody started screaming. Then,
pop! pop! Rifle fire. The police yelled, "Get down!" and
we fell to the ground.

A townie sick of PCU protests and protestors had
stolen a gun, pushed an old lady out of her car at a stoplight, drove over to city hall with the police in pursuit,
and appeared to be ready to shoot when he was shot and
killed by the police. One of the bullhorn bullies began to
cry. His girlfriend hugged him, and murmured in his ear.
I wondered fleetingly what mulishness it was in me that
relished beholding the fall of this person. I wanted to
laugh, but feared I would cry, too. The ex and I got back
on his motorcycle. I held onto him so tightly, my fingers
ached from clutching the front of his jacket. He had protected me. When we returned to campus, that obviously
stuck out in his mind, too. He seemed proud of himself.
It was probably the best time he ever had with me.

Jeff drops me off at home, where I fiddle at length

with the ranch door keys. Except for the deadbolt that was installed when two migrant workers walked right into the kitchen and held up Uncle Mas for his wallet and the keys to his truck, the locks are ancient, tended to with keys that look like those to a medieval dungeon.

Inside, one kitchen light burns. My mother and the Math are talking about the sale of the ranch. My mother sees it as a part of history. The Math views it as a commodity. How unlike my mother to be sentimental about history. As I enter the room, I notice Uncle Mas perched in one corner, not saying a word.

"How'd it go?" the Math asks. Despite the lateness of the hour, he looks like he's just gotten home. He's picking at a plate of food my mother kept warm for him. Discussing the ranch isn't an activity the Math enjoys, knowing that until there's deeper resolution between the property as history and commodity, my mother and Uncle Mas will bruit about proposals pointlessly until the end of time.

"It's eleven p.m. I'm home." I sit down. "It went like that."

"Where did you eat?" My mother wants to know.

I remove my earrings, and massage my lobes. "Someplace expensive."

"What did you have?"

"Lobster everything."

My mother goggles. "On purpose?" she asks, thinking I ordered the most expensive things on the menu deliberately, to be rude.

"He ordered."

"Then what?" my mother demands.

"Then we went dancing."

"You're home now," the Math observes.

"What's so awful?" my mother asks. "He tries to impress you, lobster everything, dancing, popular band. What's wrong with that?"

"He was a jerk." I get up. "Other than that, no problems at all."

My mother follows me into the living room. I hear Uncle Mas clomping down the porch steps toward the drive. "So ungrateful," my mother hisses, beginning to pull the drapes shut. I help her. "What boy will ever like you if you can't appreciate him?"

"I'd rather have him appreciate me," I tell my mother.

"Go to bed," she says irritably.

Headlights splash the walls momentarily as Uncle Mas, finished with his interim smoke, leaves. My mother orders me to pull the drapes along the far wall before we go blind. As I rise and do as I've been asked, I see little eyes burning bright in the dark shadows of the garden. They flash in the headlights' glare, and disappear. In one motion, I pull the curtains closed.

The Rice Eaters

The flowers my mother did for the altar and casket were discussed with my grandmother before her death. Together, they decided on homegrown chrysanthemums, white roses, and ivy. The day before the funeral, my mother worked from dawn until dusk on the casketpiece, bringing everything into the kitchen. Aunts Em and Ann helped intermittently. Uncle Mas sat at the kitchen table, opening envelopes and counting *koden*, "obituary gifts," money from friends meant to defray funeral expenses.

The morning of the funeral, Uncle Mas and the Math loaded everything into Aunt Em's Explorer. Going home from the church that night, my mother and I in the backseat, Ojiichan in front, the Math driving, my mother asked us, "How do you think it went?"

"Fine," the Math answered, loosening his tie.

"The flowers were really pretty, weren't they?" my mother pressed on in English, and when no one answered, she said to Ojiichan, in Japanese, illuminating both cultures in the words she chose, "The flowers didn't look too terrible, did they?"

Nobody answered her. At home, my mother started Ojiichan's bath, and took off her shoes and jewelry. Sitting on her bed for a moment, taking her prayer beads out of her pocketbook and putting them away in a drawer, she looked tired. She changed into a black skirt and plain blouse, and put on more lipstick. Still in their suits, Uncle Mas and the Math took up again with the *koden*. The Math booted up the computer to enter in the information: Whenever anybody dies, my mother consults the *koden* file on the computer and checks to see how much the deceased sent when my grandmother and Ojiichan died. She then relays the amount to Uncle Mas, the eldest in the family, so he knows how much to send to the family of the deceased.

Relatives began trickling in. My aunts joined Uncle Mas and the Math at the kitchen table and counted money, mostly crisp twenties, an occasional fifty. Aunts Em and Ann opened envelopes, and the Swan Girls told the Math the amounts and names of the givers. Uncle Wes lit a cigarette, and my mother told him to go out on the veranda to smoke. Uncle Sen yawned and twirled his MontBlanc pen. Uncle Mas brought out a box of Bics, and everyone scrambled around for scratch paper, scribbling to get the cheap pens going.

The Math recorded the amount, the giver, and their address on the computer. Anyone who didn't have anything to do wrote thank you notes on stationery selected by my grandmother, ecru cards with a purple Dharma wheel on the front. "Your kindness will always be remembered." Uncle Sen signed his own name, "Sentaro," until Uncle Mas saw and told him to start over, using the family name.

My mother made several pots of tea. Her friend Cheryl counted heads. The Gotandas brought a platter of sushi, so my mother wouldn't have to cook the next day. The Math's mother's side of the family came from Osno, and huddled together clannishly in the living room. Ojiichan's brother's children, all in their forties and fifties, got in everyone's way until they were seated in the dining room. Reverend Matsunaga stopped in with his wife, and the Math brought down a set of my grandmother's tea cups from the Shaker cabinet's high pantry. The Swan Girls cut and served two cakes someone had brought from Charlie's Bakery. Ojiichan came out in his pajamas, had a piece of cake with Reverend Matsunaga, and went to bed.

People started telling cancer stories. They compared oncologists, hospitals, and insurance. They debated surgery, chemotherapy, and holistic practices. They talked about relatives in Japan afflicted with cancer, and Japanese socialized medicine. Uncle Sen opined that socialism breeds mediocrity, and somebody else refuted that, saying, "Only in a mediocre society."

"Look around, fool," Uncle Sen snorted. "Ann! More tea."

Conversation was diverted to health plans. The Swan Girls offered around second servings of cake and tea. My mother brought out three rolls of stamps, and cut up a sponge for moisteners. The Math kept the computer clicking with names, numbers, and addresses.

At the end of the evening, only Uncles Mas and Sen, Aunts Em and Ann, my mother, the Math, and I remained. The women wrote thank yous. Uncle Mas stamped them. The Math finished up the last of the cake. Uncle Sen studied my grandmother's funeral program, discussed long in advance with my mother.

" 'Ben Okado,' " he read. "Who was that?"

"Pallbearer," my mother said, washing dishes. I was helping her, drying them and putting them away.

"Cut the obvious. Betty Okado's son?"

"Perk and Betty's grandson."

Uncle Sen tossed the program aside. "Whose idea was that?"

"Mama's," my mother said, rinsing a plate. "So don't start."

"Start what?" Uncle Sen asked, and went on: "All the Okados ever brought Mama was trouble. Dunno why she would want one of them to carry her to her grave."

This was true. In camp, Betty Okado slapped my grandmother with a wet sheet. Awkward in her eighth month of pregnancy, my grandmother fell into the rows of troughs behind her, and went into early labor. The twin girls died.

"That's what she wanted," my mother said. "Perk Okado did a lot for us."

"That low-life gambler," Uncle Sen said.

"Lots of Issei men gambled," my mother said irritably.

"Who lost the family restaurant to a four-of-a-kind?" Uncle Sen asked, referring to Perk Okado's legendary loss of his chop suey diner to an out-of-towner. "Lemme see that again," Uncle Sen ordered, picking up the funeral program. "No other choice for pallbearer, huh? What about the Akiyamas?"

My mother's voice grew cold. "If you thought it should have been otherwise, you should have helped plan the funeral."

"Jesus Christ," Uncle Sen said. "Why don'tcha blame Masa? He didn't help you neither, and he was the real reason Mama lost those girls, going away at seventeen, the way he did. That was when things went bad for her, alluva sudden."

Uncle Mas, and everybody else, blinked. "That's a lie," my mother said. "Masa had nothing to do with any of that. You may as well blame Papa, for signing Mama's citizenship away. That was when things started to go bad for her."

"You benefitted the most," Uncle Sen said piercingly. My mother turned to face him, letting her wet hands drip into the sink. "It would have been different for you, if those girls lived."

"Hush, Sen," Aunt Ann said. He shook her hand off his arm.

"*Urusai*," Aunt Em complained. Shut up.

"Boy," Uncle Mas said, not missing a stamp. "Yak yak yak."

I laughed. My mother turned to me, and took the cloth I held. "I'll finish up," she said, drying her hands. "Go check Ojiichan's nightlight, and go to bed."

"I don't mind," I said, meaning I wanted to stay.

"Good night," she said forcefully, then added, "and brush your teeth well after all that cake."

I swizzled my tongue around in my mouth as I hurried away. Regretting I had drawn attention to myself, I went to Ojiichan's room. He was asleep, snoring heavily. He had plugged in his nightlight himself. I crept in, and laid down on the floor with my ear to the vent. Despite Ojiichan snoring loudly, I could hear the conversation in the kitchen as though I was there.

A year after being taken from his home in California, Ojiichan joined his family in the camp. He regained some limited freedom. Even after leaving camp, though, he had to report to a parole officer every six weeks. This went on until the end of the war. It was like being a criminal, a concept that offended his conservative sensibilities to their core. He blamed his battered pride, shredded on the American barbed wire surrounding him and his family, and the Japanese for bombing America, casting themselves, and by extension him, in such a negative light.

In 1943, the government handed out questionnaires to all internees. Questions 27 and 28 read: "Would you be willing to serve in the armed forces on combat duty, wherever ordered?" and "Will you swear to unqualified allegiance and faithfully defend the United States, foreswearing any form of allegiance or obedience to the Japanese emperor?"

The questionnaires were designed to weed out Japanese loyalists for deportation. Older Japanese, those without American citizenship, panicked. To answer "yes" to both meant to be formally without a country. Rumors flew around camp that dissenters were being shot, pro-Japan groups were waiting to terrorize those who failed to dissent, and America planned to ship all the Japanese to Japan after the war anyway, regardless of what was said.

Ojiichan was resolute in his American loyalties. Certain he would one day be allowed to become a citizen, he answered "yes" to both questions without hesitation, first in his own form, and when she opposed him, on his wife's as well.

That was what my mother had meant by Ojiichan signing away my grandmother's citizenship. He didn't give her a choice, and he didn't give Uncle Mas a choice, either.

Uncle Mas was thirteen going on fourteen when the war began, sixteen when the U.S. Army formed the all-Nisei—second generation—combat unit, the 442nd, and seventeen when Ojiichan helped him decide that he wanted to join up. Ojiichan signed the consent papers, and Uncle Mas was off to Anzio.

My grandmother was horrified, and she was called unpatriotic as a result. From one block to the next, everyone knew everything. In the eyes of the pro-American Issei and Nisei with whom she lived in flimsy tarpaper shacks, she had committed treason. She was snubbed in the latrine lines, and during arts and crafts in the rec hall. Other mothers of 442nd volunteers refused to acknowledge her.

Betty Okado took the opposite tack, assaulting her. Her own son was one of the first killed in battle. Betty hadn't been the same since her house in Oakland was burned, her husband taken in for questioning, her eldest son killed in the Italian Alps. Since there were no washing facilities in the camp, the sinks in which hands were washed and used toothpaste was spat served as laundry basins. Betty saw my grandmother while they were doing their laundry, they exchanged words, and Betty slapped her with a heavy, wet sheet. It was the summer of 1944. The following morning, amid cries of joy from all corners of the camp at the news that Roosevelt had revoked his edict and the Japanese could return to the west coast, my grandmother delivered two premature girls with critical respiratory problems.

The medical facilities at the camp were such that the doctor, the same one who operated on Uncle Mas years earlier, hadn't known that my grandmother was carrying twins. He didn't expect them to live past the end of the month, maybe the week. They could have been taken to a more adequate hospital outside the fences, but none would take Japanese babies, even American ones.

Around then, Ojiichan proudly announced to the family that they would be among the first to leave the camp. They would be out in a matter of weeks, headed for their sponsors in Colorado. Ojiichan cast a worried eye at his new daughters, already envisioning the future drain on the family's barren coffers. These girls, not expected to live, wouldn't even survive the train ride out of camp. Ojiichan thought about funerals, and cost, and finding a mortuary that would accept Japanese. Burials cost money. Girls were regarded as a poor investment with minimal return anyway; they eventually left their birth families and married into others.

Ojiichan wasn't mercenary, but he was sensible. He related everything to business. Prior to the war, he had owned a bait shop, and, unusual for Japanese merchants at the time, he ran an aggressive ad campaign on the radio.

It featured a jingle he somehow wrote himself, called, "Catch the Fish You Wish":

> *To catch the fish you wish*
> *Without any hesitation or ado*
> *Hurry to the Wish Bait Shop*
> *Where all your dreams come true.*

"All fishermen, they big dreamers," Ojiichan explained of his success. "Will use anything, do anything, get that big fish. Japanese, white, never make no difference, they all got one thing in common." He stabbed at the air with his cigarette. "Everyone got big hope."

Ojiichan never rested until he was very old, and by then it was the only option his family, on some level tired of his infinite energy, availed to him in the form of a La-Z-Boy and a remote control. In the camp hospital, my grandmother said they should stay. The babies would be taken care of for as long as necessary, and Uncle Mas, in Italy then, would know his family was safe from "Jap haters." The government had locked up the Japanese for the safety of national security, but some believed the camps had better served the safety of the Japanese.

Ojiichan believed neither. Throughout his life, he talked about being grateful to be in America, humiliated to have necessitated suspicion during the war, and anxious to repay his debt to American society. All his life, he was deeply driven to prove himself worthy. Even with the war still on and heavy losses in the Pacific, he wanted to get out of camp as soon as possible. Anti-American sentiment never bothered him the way it bothered my grandmother.

She worried on behalf of her children. Ojiichan waved his hand in the face of her fears.

"They have to suffer to be strong," he said in Japanese. "They have to give back to America, not take more."

My grandmother was in no condition to give anything back to anyone. Her daughters were dying. When they listened to the rec hall radio to hear about the war effort, her other children yelled, "Hit 'em again!" Her husband talked about the debt they owed the country that had imprisoned them. The only thing she felt empowered to give was mercy. The night before they left for Colorado, she crept down to the nursery and smothered her daughters to death with a pillow while they slept. The official cause of death was respiratory failure. The government handled the burial, putting the girls in the ground a few hundred yards outside the fence. In death, they did what they couldn't do during their lives: leave the camp.

"Shut up, Sen," I heard my mother say. "That didn't happen."

"Tell me what happened then," he mocked her.

"Their lungs were weak. Mama would kill you. She hated your kind of talk."

My mother would know. From the beginning, my grandmother and mother were very close. My mother had pneumonia twice between the ages of four and six. It was probably due to the drafty chicken coop, but each time she got sick, my grandmother was terrified her daughter would die of causes no doctor could specify, and she herself couldn't articulate. She felt that this was her punishment for stealing the air from her twins' lungs. What greater torture than my grandmother's penalty visited on the daughter that got to live?

It was while my mother was sick that my grandmother developed her oppressive conviction that she would die early, of a disease in her lungs. Nearly a baby herself when her twin sisters were born and died, all her life my mother got enough attention from her mother for three girls. My grandmother willed that her daughter would be her opposite: In every thought, word, and deed, her daughter would be beautiful, dutiful, and good. *Perfect* is the most punitive word in the English language. Hell doesn't even come close. My mother is shackled by her obligation to perfection like a woman in chains of iron.

"You think you run everything so smooth," Uncle Sen sneered. "You think you find ways to organize mortal chaos, managing Mama's funeral. Ava, where do you get this idea, you can change the truth?"

"This has been a long day for everybody," my mother said. "I bet I can forgive you tomorrow, though."

I scrambled up, hurried from Ojiichan's room to my own, and jumped in bed to my neck, fully clothed. My mother came in a moment later, smelling like anger, roses, and lemon verbena soap. "Are you awake?" she asked, peering at me in the sliver of hall light.

"Yes," I said.

"You should be asleep." Three roses, leftover from my grandmother's funeral flowers, were in her hand. She broke off the stems, and put them in the trash.

"I checked Ojiichan's light."

"Good." She took the roses she was twisting and put them on my bedside table. "Get a blanket from the closet if you get cold tonight," she said.

My mother spent the rest of the night finishing the *koden* herself. I could hear her in the kitchen, after everybody else had gone home. The Math had gone to bed. The same way it echoed in the heating duct, Uncle Sen's phrase, "organizing mortal chaos," echoed in my head. That morning, in the kitchen, I had heard my mother muse to Uncle Mas, "When your parents die, you're really an adult." Uncle Mas said nothing, and I wondered, How could she ever be anything else? The phrase "Time is a wheel" made me shiver. Suddenly, I wished I had told my mother I liked the flowers when she had asked in the car.

The funeral was ideal, the flowers beautiful. In my room my eyes were drawn to my bedside table. My grandmother's roses shone bright white in the dark, a special nightlight just for me.

Garden of Pearls

~~~~~~~~~~

At the grocery, in the freezer section, my mother and I run into Mrs. Sato. She's the same age Ojiichan would have been, and they came from the same prefecture in Japan. She looks ancient until she smiles, revealing a toothless cavity. Then she looks like a happy child awaiting a windfall from the tooth fairy. I peek into her cart, which is as tall as she is. She's buying a quart of lactose-reduced milk, frozen spinach, and seven Hungry Man TV dinners, which, I happen to know, she eats with a full bowl of rice every night. Issei generally don't like milk, but Mrs. Sato has osteoporosis, has her bone deterioration monitored regularly, drinks a glass of milk every morning, and takes calcium supplements. My mother whispers all this to me once Mrs. Sato and her cart round the corner, shuffling toward produce.

My mother fills two carts full. "Plastic, Ma'am?" The bag boy loads up our groceries, and tells me, "Most people switched over to paper, but not your ma. She recycles these plastic bags."

I bet she hasn't told him what she recycles them as. "She's pretty economical," I agree.

"Your ma never lets me take her bags out to the car. She always does it herself, so I don't even offer anymore."

"That's how she is."

"I have my daughter with me today," my mother says, putting her change in her purse and heading out to the parking lot without looking back.

I push the cart. The parking lot reflects the town, full of family wagons, luxury cars, and a few sports models driven by suburban fathers subliminally indulging midlife crises. As I look around, the cart bumps my mother's heels, and she glares over her shoulder at me.

I slow down. "Sorry."

Today we're driving the little Honda rice rocket my parents bought as a "third car," a spare. It's a white hatchback, license plate, MI HUEVO: Occasionally, my mother is possessed by a fleeting fragment of humor. She opens the trunk, and I heft two bags. "We have to get a present for your father to take to Osno this weekend."

My mother's family isn't such a bargain, but the Math's family makes Uncles Mas, Sen, Wes, and company look desirable. The Math's mother's family's reunions fill stadiums and stacks of photo albums. The Math's mother had a huge passel of siblings, who have multiplied like rabbits over the years. The lot of them were born in and reside in Osno, a town of stop lights, gas stations/mini-marts, rental storage facilities, discount appliance stores, and fast-food restaurants laid out like a grid in the center of an arid plain.

A few of the Osno group escaped to L.A. They learned to walk upright, but an Osno family stamp has lingered, a birthmark of birthplace: They're all educated, which is both their best and worst feature. Japanese Americans typically love learning, but the Osno group is obsessed. Uncles Mas and Sen never went to college. After my grandmother's funeral, Uncle Sen asked Uncle Mas, "Who the hell are those people?" Later, we heard that one of the Math's cousins had asked Uncle Sen if he had ever thought about returning to school to get a degree.

Without exception, the Osno group all go to college, even the Social Security set. They're totally consumed with school as a means of self-improvement. This dedication has borne surprisingly meager fruit, partly because they all wind up at Osno State majoring in engineering or physical therapy, mostly because they go to school but are afflicted with a poverty of intellect. Education for education's sake leaves them cold. What's the point, if the degree isn't a shiny bauble to yo-yo with abandon in the faces of others?

"No sooner do we look away than one of the Osno bunch is getting married, having a baby, graduating from school, retiring, or dropping dead," I grumble as my mother starts the car.

"There are sure a lot of them," my mother agrees.

The Osno group's invitations to weddings, baby showers, and birthday, graduation, and retirement parties crowd the mailbox often. The Math enjoys his relatives. He says they can't help the way they are. He's the eldest cousin, only a few years younger than his mother's youngest sister, who is throwing a birthday party for her new granddaughter this weekend. My mother and I set out to buy a present for the little hostage to fortune.

"How about Candyland," my mother muses at the mall.

"I was going to suggest a lifetime therapy gift certificate."

We settle on a red ensemble. Matching socks come with it. Afterward, we both get sodas at the Food Bazaar, a chain of dining dioramas with all the major world cuisines represented: Chinese, Italian, Mexican, Greek, Japanese, French, and Pronto Pups. As we're seated, I roll my cup of cold soda over my brow, beads of moisture cooling my skin. My mother gives me a disapproving look, her eyes rolling upward as she sucks daintily on her straw.

"I've been so tired," I complain, patting myself with my napkin. "I think it's the heat."

"The doctor said that might be a side effect."

"Being tired?"

"And heat," she says. "He said, drink liquids."

"I do," I affirm, and pause. "I was getting a soda at the hospital the other day, when we checked in Uncle Sen and I ran into a friend from PCU."

"We've got that roast in the car," my mother says. "We should go."

In the car, my mother hums along with her oldies radio station, tapping her hands on the steering wheel, usually out of sync with the beat. I don't notice that we're driving toward the hills until it's too late. Ann Sayles's brick two-story looms in the window. Gravel crackles and pops beneath our tires. My mother turns the engine off, and fixes her lipstick in the rearview mirror.

"I thought we were going home."

"I just picked up some things for Mother Sayles."

Mother Sayles: I make a face. "I'll wait here."

"She always looks out her window as I drive away," my mother says. "What would she think if she saw you sitting here?"

"It only matters if I care."

Belaboring the obvious, I hear, "I care." My mother puts her lipstick back in her purse, and asks me, "Have I mentioned before that she's very sick?"

Amelia—the maid—answers the door. Amelia is short, dumpy, and doesn't speak any English. I've never met her before, but she doesn't differ much from the last Amelia. Ann Sayles has called all her "girls" Amelia, beginning with my grandmother. As a child, Ann Sayles always envisioned herself attended to by a servant named Amelia. Since her marriage, she has had a succession of Amelias. In this fashion, she never has to learn a strange foreign name. During the heyday of her entertaining years, when her children still lived at home and her husband was professor emeritus at the nearby university, she had two Amelias, and called the second one Annie. This Amelia leads us into the parlor, and takes the bag my mother brought in.

"Please refrigerate that," my mother says. She sinks into a velvet chair, making a series of empty gestures. "Refrigerate?"

"Can't Amelia drive?" I ask after she leaves. "Why are you bringing food?"

"Better bargains at Cala," my mother says, and before I have a chance to point out that Ann Sayles's house is twenty minutes out of our way—no bargain there—my mother smooths her skirt and stands.

"Ava," Ann Sayles says weakly, leaning in the doorway with her walker. "Wilhelmina, my pretty dear. What a nice surprise."

My mother goes to her, I study my hands, and flex my fingers experimentally. Suddenly, I share my mother's distaste for eye contact. While my mother helps seat Ann Sayles on the plush camel couch, I pick a little scab off my palm. Moving my PCU boxes around, one of the corners gouged me, but I heal fast. At twenty, time is a friend to me. Laughably, its only unkindness is the byproduct of my impatience: It seems to move so slowly.

It isn't the first time, but it is by far the most vivid: Looking at Ann Sayles, I see that terminal illness is a crevasse in the granite of time, and youth really is wasted on the young. The last time I saw her, she looked as she always has. Since then, her patrician features have sunken and shriveled to a hodgepodge of runes and raisins, and she is aware of it. Her formerly iron-clad arrogance has dwindled to a nervous self-consciousness. She has developed a repertoire of new gestures that give her away, touching what remains of the hair that is the biggest surprise: It has gone back to nature, and she even makes reference to her startling lack of color and coiffure.

"I can't make it to the beauty parlor anymore," she says, compulsively tweaking her gray strands, smoothing them, then exciting them to a vertical stance again with jittery fingertips. Her rings are the only thing about her that sparkle with life. "Alas, now that I most need it," she adds plaintively.

"You need to rest," my mother says in a voice so loud I jump, and in this way, I learn that Ann Sayles has lost some ground in at least one of her five senses. "You'll be fine! Good as new!"

"Well," she laughs a little, "the dogs bark."

"You'll be fine," my mother caws.

Ann Sayles directs her attention to me. "How old are you now, my dear?"

"Twenty," I shout.

"My, so young," Ann Sayles says. She seems to find this humorous, and chuckles. Her whole demeanor is incongruently light, as though any minute she might float up to the sky on balloons of mirth and rue. "You must have many beaux."

"No!"

"Twenty." Ann Sayles nods. "Indeed, I believe that was how old your grandmother was when she came to work for me."

"I'm graduating from college next summer," I holler. "I'll send you a résumé."

She leans. "What was that last?"

"Nothing," my mother says, and her voice cracks around the edges. "We have to be going!"

"Did you bring any of your delightful arrangements today, Ava?" Ann Sayles asks, looking around. "They so brighten a gloomy room, and my house seems full of gloomy rooms since I took sick."

"I plan to work in the garden tomorrow," my mother shouts, hand to her throat. She hates to raise her voice. "We've been so busy with family matters this week."

"I can well imagine, with Wilhelmina home," Ann Sayles smiles at me.

"Maybe I'll stop by later in the week," my mother says.

"I would like that. How much do I owe you, Ava? For the groceries?"

"Oh, nothing, Mother Sayles." My mother stands. "It wasn't much."

"Nonsense. Amelia!" she bawls and rings the bell on a side table. I wonder if my grandmother heard and heeded that ringing bell. Ann Sayles fumbles with it. My mother helps her set it upright on the table. Ann Sayles giggles, flexing her arthritic fingers. Amelia brings her pocketbook. "Now, how much did you say it came to, my dear?"

"No, no, I insist," my mother says.

"Isn't she cute?" Ann Sayles asks me. "Isn't she charming?"

"About twelve, thirteen dollars," I tell her, and my mother kicks me in the ankle.

She rummages around in her wallet and comes up with a ten and a twenty. She proffers the ten. My mother accepts the bill and a kiss on the cheek. With an unsteady hand laden with those huge rings, Ann Sayles pats her shoulder, and her rheumy old eyes find mine, and crinkle.

"See you again, my dear."

As we roll out of the driveway, Ann Sayles waves us away from her window, just the way my mother said she would. I've subsided in a sulk when my mother brakes rashly and pulls to the side of the road.

"What," I say, but my mother isn't focused on me.

"Look," she says, and I do. Crows wheel in the sky, right over the road. After a car passes, they swoop down, then fly away. They're dropping things on the road, picking them up again, and wheeling away.

"What are they doing?" I ask, squinting.

"Eating," my mother says. "See those almond trees?"

A row of almond trees line the road, behind a fence. The crows are taking the almonds, dropping them in the road, and waiting for cars to come and crush the shells. If a few cars pass by without results, the crows reposition the almond on the road, and wait again in the sky.

"What did crows used to do, before cars?" my mother wonders, and she looks pleased and interested as she pulls out into traffic again. "Incredible."

Watching her profile, I'm thinking the same of her. The women in my family agree it's first loves and children that break a heart worse than anyone. I don't know why nobody ever said the same for parents.

Uncle Mas helps unload the car. My mother prattles on about running into Mrs. Sato, new construction at the corner of Milk Run Road and Fifth, and the price of rib eye. I wash an apple, and take it to my room. On my bed is the dress my grandmother made for my mother to wear in Uncle Sen and Aunt Ann's wedding, my high school prom dress. I took it out of the closet before my date. Now I think I might wear it for my birthday dinner. I grasp my apple in my teeth, disrobe, and pull the dress over my head. It pulls a little, and I hear a few pearls pop off the neckline. The delicate starburst design is already missing pearls here and there, but it's a pretty dress. I turn this way and that, rattling the fallen pearls in my hand. My mother appears in the mirror behind me.

"I'll be in the kitchen," she says. "After all this time, Uncle Mas still doesn't know where anything goes."

"Okay."

"Later, I'll rebait the badger traps."

"New bait?"

"The old stuff doesn't work. This is my last hope." She comes in. "You should cut those threads," she says, motioning to the dress. "They'll get snagged. The sewing scissors are in the junk drawer, unless someone took them somewhere."

"I'll find them." I turn away from the mirror, think to change out of the dress, and pause. "Age is a tough break," I observe finally, thinking of Ann Sayles.

"Mrs. Sato has a hearty constitution," my mother says. "She should show you the moxa scars on her back sometime." Moxa is Japanese medicine. A lot of older Japanese have scars the size of silver dollars on their bodies, where moxa was burned to relieve pain. Someone Mrs. Sato's age would have a lot of scars.

My mother glances around. "You know, I vacuumed in here before you came home."

"Thanks."

"I wish you would put on slippers. Less wear for the carpet." With that, she vanishes down the hall, and I hear her moving around in the kitchen.

I ease out of the dress, change, and sit on my bed a moment, my gaze cast upon the mountain of books by the door. Somewhere in that pile, there's got to be a secret equation that would unlock my mother to me if I knew it, a mineral that works magic on ailing relationships, or a rare herb that cures at first taste. That which I envision, I don't know where to look for it, or even how to begin. I get up, straighten my shorts, and take the dress downstairs, mindful of its pearls and fragility.

The scissors are where they're supposed to be, and I take them out onto the veranda with the dress. It smells like autumn even though it's still summer. Sitting on the steps, I cut, and accidentally unravel the thread that strands together a sweeping starburst of pearls! They go bouncing down the walk and into the grass in a great release, and trying frantically to stop them with my feet is of no use. With an attendant chorus of cartwheeling acorns, the pearls ricochet and chatter like gumballs or hail.

My mother comes running. "What was that? Oh, Wil," she says when she sees. She drops to her knees beside me to better inspect the damage. "Mama's design."

"It was an accident."

"She sewed that herself."

I turn. "I was just cutting the threads." I set down the scissors, like a gunman surrendering a weapon. My mother shakes her head. "All I did was cut a thread," I repeat, backing away to flee into the house's cool repose. "It was just an accident. I didn't mean to do any harm."

Careless Hands

~~~~~~~~~~

"**D**arn these gophers," my mother says, circling the southwest side of the garden, checking her traps. The lawn is dotted with plastic grocery bags, into which she stuffs dead gophers for quick burial. Later, before darkness falls, she or I will push the wheelbarrow around and collect the carcasses. I can imagine how we must look to the uninitiated, or from an aerial view. My mother carries a short club, in case the gopher hasn't had the courtesy to expire before she comes across it. This became standard operating procedure after she caught what seemed to be a dead possum in a trap. She threw the possum in a bag, and tossed the bag in a garbage can. A few days later, taking out the trash, she lifted the lid, and the possum was standing up, looking around. She slammed the lid down. The Math explained that there's a chemical in possums that enables them to seem to "sleep," hence the phrase, "playing possum."

My mother expertly springs a trap open, extracts the gopher, and pops it in a plastic bag. In a few economical gestures, she ties the handles, tosses the bag a few feet, and resets the trap. She glances over at the jewel flowers I'm watering. "What junk," is her verdict. She pushes her bonnet back on her head, and squints to see. "Don't waste water. Those are nothing but weeds."

"They're pretty." I go to turn off the tap.

Uncle Mas sits on the veranda nearby, spitting pumpkin seed shells out the screen door. The pumpkins were grown and the seeds roasted here at the ranch. Uncle Mas's chair is angled to the side, so I can't see him. His shells come shooting out onto the stairs and walkway. Pearls from yesterday dot the lawn. Uncle Mas has a cup of green tea, and an Idaho paper folded back to the real estate and classified ads. I turn my head to listen, but he's still. Anyway, it's impossible to hear much over the nightly chorus of cicadas. The paper rattles faintly, and I smell smoke. I fidget, letting the hose drop out of my hand to the walkway as I chase the mosquitoes away from my arms and neck. Uncle Mas is convinced that smoking keeps the bugs away from him; his blood tastes too bad for them to bite him.

The driveway curves around the house on three sides. Rough L-shaped walks divide the garden at two corners of the yard. Both begin on the west side of the driveway, one curving to the north, the other to the south.

The one that curves to the north goes by the veranda. When she was alive, every night toward sundown my grandmother would shell almonds, clean shrimp, peel apples. The Swan Girls and I played in the northwest triangle of the garden, bordered by the narrow walkway. We chalked hopscotch grids on the concrete. My grandmother watched us from the veranda, her hands busy. Going into the house to use the bathroom, I squint at Uncle Mas. The sun should illuminate the veranda, but the heavy screens shadow it black.

"What," he says in the darkness.

Yesterday, after the dress debacle, I thought it best to stay well out of my mother's sightline. I went to find the bassinette for Hope, but it was gone, as were boxes of the Swan Girls' baby things, clothes, and toys and such. Earlier, I had seen Uncle Mas leaving the ranch with a box as big as he was. When I asked, he said he was going to the post office.

I shade my eyes. "Anything interesting in the paper?"

"Jobs."

"You looking for a job?"

"Nope."

I lean on one leg, stretching my hamstrings. They feel as though they're all bunched up behind my knee after a full day working outside. "What kind of jobs?"

"Fishing expeditions."

I stretch the other leg. "Up in Idaho?" When he affirms this, I say, "Sometimes people get different jobs after retirement." I try to picture Uncle Mas in a tricorn hat, flipping burgers and asking, "Fries, to go?" "You have plenty of fishing experience."

His monotone turns faintly agitated. He slurps his tea. "Flight fishing expeditions," he says.

"In a plane?"

His cup clinks against the glass tabletop as he sets it down. There's a rustle of newspaper, and Uncle Mas reads: " 'Help wanted: Pilot/handyman to fly and maintain small Cessna, rivers inaccessible by road. Six days a week in high season, off December–March. Fishing experience preferred.' " The paper snaps closed. "Benefits, too."

This is probably the most I've ever heard him say at one time. I slap at the back of my neck, and scratch. "That would be something," I say at last, though privately, I have doubts. One summer, Uncle Mas and Aunt Em took all the Swan Girls and me to Disneyland. Uncle Mas threw up after a polish sausage and the Flying Teacups.

"Yeah," Uncle Mas says. "Something."

"If you want to learn to fly," I tell him, "you probably could."

"Nope," he says. "Too old."

"Have you seen Ann Sayles lately?"

"Who? Oh, her? Nope."

I shake my legs out, brushing away mosquitoes. "What about Mrs. Sato?"

"Still alive?"

"We saw her at the grocery yesterday."

"Osteo . . . osteo . . ."

"Sure, but Mrs. Sato is ninety-whatever and still driving herself to the store. She has a good appetite, too. And Ann Sayles still tortures Mom like a pro. You should think about utilizing the second half of your life for something worthwhile," I tell him.

"Second half," he scoffs. "Fourth fifth. Maybe, third fourth."

"Well, let's not make a movie out of the fractions."

"Movie?"

"The girls are grown and gone, and you're retired." I hesitate, and after finding the words off in the middle distance where I gaze, I finally suggest, "Hanging around the ranch all the time, maybe you get bored."

"Not bored."

"Well," I allow dubiously, "you know what I mean."

When he doesn't say anything, I go inside, and use the bathroom. I flush, and hear my mother call, "Wil! Masa!"

I step outside. "Where are you?"

"Here! Hurry!"

I go around the south side of the house. Uncle Mas and my mother are standing over one of her traps. "Look at this," she says, excited. "Come see."

She's caught the badger. It's alive, but its fleas are already jumping off. Fleas and doctors always know when the body is going to go cold. My mother and Uncle Mas loom over the badger. Its leg, by which it's caught in the trap, trembles in a blur.

I bend over it too, fascinated. "I've never seen a badger up close before," I whisper.

"We usually just have gophers." My mother peers at it. "I don't know where this guy came from."

"Not normal," Uncle Mas agrees.

"I always thought badgers were a kind of raccoon." I get closer. "Gee, is that what marmots look like?"

"I don't know," my mother says. "But I thought

you would want to see it." And with one swift gesture, she clubs it over the head. Her hit sounds solid. She has a good arm. Something breaks. It sounds pretty bad. The badger squeals, and spasms. It cries out, and there are great tears welling in its bright, black eyes. So my mother hits it again, harder.

My heart thunders in my mouth. I look at my mother, then Uncle Mas, and then turn away so I don't throw up all over my mother's quarry.

"Wow, big," my mother notes to Uncle Mas, slightly breathless. In her competent way, she springs the jaws of her trap open. "Look at his paws. Those sharp claws, digging up all my hard work. Go get a Hefty bag, Wil. Look in the entryway pantry." I fumble-foot a little, backing toward the house. "Hurry up," she says impatiently. "Flies will come. Look at his paws," she marvels again to Uncle Mas, holding one up with the head of her club.

"Big," he nods.

I go inside, past the entryway, and hurry into the bathroom before I throw up. All the blood has rushed to my head, making my cheeks burn. Leaning against the toilet, my hands shake. I wash my face, and blow my nose. I think of my mother saying many times over the years, "Crying never helped anybody, and it never brought anybody back. So blow your nose."

I shake a Hefty bag loose from the big Price Club box and go out the back door, around the house. My mother is standing on the walkway, waiting for me. "I thought you would come out the side door. Give me," she says, opening and closing her hand impatiently. I hand her the bag. She drops the dead badger in with a hideous thunk, and tugs the drawstrings closed. Once they're tied in a knot, she swings the bag onto the lawn. I wince at the noise this careless movement makes, and my fingers ball into fists.

"The sun sets earlier and earlier," she observes, pushing her hat back with her forearm. "Next thing you know, it's going to be winter." She surveys her domain. "I have a lot of work to do before then."

"Where did Uncle Mas go?" I ask her.

"Isn't he in the house?" She starts toward the veranda, stepping over the hose. "Recoil this, would you? Someone is going to fall and break their head open."

I pick up the hose, from the head. It loops and tangles up the walkway. Water reactivates the faint smell of puke on my hands, which tremble; my fingernails had cut half moons in my palms. The garden looks like the inside of a persimmon, filled with dark orange light. My mother strips off her gloves, and steps carefully over the hose. She's been out in the sun all day, but a soft square of white neck bobs above her collar. I want to throw up again. Instead, when my mother's foot is in a hose loop, I yank the hose up in a coil around my hand.

Her arms pinwheel, and she lets out a yelp as she falls backward. A sharp cracking sound resonates around us as her head hits the pavement. When I rush to her, skinning my knee and popping something in it in my hurry to kneel, a deep grimace is scrawled over her face. Her fingers scratch at the concrete. She groans.

The cicadas are deafening. Her forehead works. "Who? You win," she mumbles. She jerks her shoulder away when I touch her, and I pull back equally. "Who?" she says, her voice going high. "You win."

And I smell sunlight, and a hint of her lemony soap, and I whisper, "We're on the same side."

Memory is associative, fragile links in a weblike configuration in every brain. Working in the garden with my mother, I'm always drawn to the jewel flowers. Nobody seems to know what their English name is; "jewel flowers" is the translation. They smell a little like snapdragons, sweet as honey and candy, which is curious considering the story behind them.

Once there was a king, and as his pregnant wife brought him his breakfast, she loudly broke wind. The king was enraged that his wife should be so indelicate and had her banished from the kingdom.

In the village of her childhood, she gave birth to a boy. He grew up to be tall and handsome. In his mother's adoring eyes, his only flaw was his constant questioning who his father was. She would say nothing except that he was a very powerful man.

Finally, one of the old aunties in the village told him to look in his mother's bedding for the jewel with six sides to it. With that jewel, golden flowers would grow. They would cure all ills, promising to he who possessed the jewel a long, healthy life.

The boy found the jewel, so the mother told him her story: He was the son of the king. He asked his mother for the jewel, and set off for the palace in which his father lived. At the gate, he cried: "I have the jewel that grows the golden flowers!"

The king tried to ignore him, but the boy persisted. Finally, he was summoned by servants of the king. He entered the palace through the nobles' entrance.

The king allowed him an audience. "Have you really the jewel from which the golden flowers grow?" he asked.

The boy held it aloft. "I have," he said. "But unless it's tended to by a woman who never breaks wind, the jewel will not bloom."

The king was infuriated. "How can you ask such a thing? How can that be!" he cried. "You fool! There is no woman on earth who never breaks wind!"

"Then why did you drive my mother away?" the boy asked.

In light of this logic, the king relented, and allowed his mother back. In time, the boy became the king himself, and with the jewel that grew the golden flowers, enjoyed a long, healthy life.

"Double play," the Math says glumly at the hospital. He means that Uncle Sen is on the floor above my mother. "This is awful. Let's go outside and find Masa. Tell me again what happened."

"I don't know. What did the doctor say?"

"She'll be fine," the Math assures me, steering me toward the elevator. "It's called a subdural hematoma."

"God," I exhale.

"What happened, Wil?" he asks, holding the elevator door open for me.

I eye the intern sharing the elevator with us. When she smiles at me, I look away. "I don't know," I whisper.

"What?" the Math demands.

"I don't know what happened. She fell."

"She tripped?"

"I'm not sure."

We exit the elevator ahead of the young woman we rode down with, walk a few corridors, and come to the front entrance. The Math had a paper to deliver tonight, in the city, cocktails and dinner after. "She fell," he prompts.

"The hose."

"The hose got coiled around her leg, she twisted her ankle? What?" The Math loosens his tie, and looks around for Uncle Mas. "Was it like this?" He pivots, and I almost laugh.

"No! I said, I don't know."

"Christ, Mina. Hey, Masa." The Math turns to Uncle Mas, who had gone outside for a cigarette. "You were probably sitting out on the veranda. What happened?"

"Didn't see," Uncle Mas says. When my mother screamed, he came out of the front door, on the south side of the house. But when I look to him now, he casts his cigarette butt down on the pavement and walks away.

Uncle Icarus

Displayed around the room he shares with a fellow recovering alcoholic—a young guy in a silk robe and a "Recovering Catholic" t-shirt—Uncle Sen is surrounded by flowers my mother brought before she joined him here, blooms in various stages of decline. References to God decorate all four walls, and Uncle Sen's recent efforts in structural art therapy occupy most of the horizontal space. The main idea behind structural art therapy is the same as that guiding traditional art therapy, but it uses three-dimensional form. "Your uncle is one of our most creative artisans," one of the nurses tells me when she brings Uncle Sen a fresh pitcher of water and a tablespoon of honey. The honey is an hourly ritual meant to keep Uncle Sen's blood sugar level stable. After so many years of a diet that might as well have consisted of two hundred Mars bars a day, he needs all the help attaining stability he can get.

Uncle Sen negates the nurse's praise but seems pleased to show me his styrofoam life preserver, for people with a lake of fire on their immortal agenda. The nurse reads the title aloud, "The SS Asbestos," and Uncle Sen cracks a smile. The godly atmosphere in this place must be getting to him. Not ordinarily one to indulge in flighty financial schemes for myself or others, I hear myself telling him he should market the preservers as money-making novelty items.

"Creativity," Uncle Sen gripes in the nurse's wake, putting the life preserver aside. "More like survival."

I indicate the discarded floatation device. "With adequate promotion, you could be on to something big."

He brightens a little. "Religious leaders could provide the hot air for inflation," Uncle Sen reasons, after a minute. "But when it cools, that's a problem." He eases back. "That sinking feeling!"

"It's the ultimate test of faith."

Uncle Sen owns a copy of the bible. It's in two rococo volumes, Old and New Testaments. The bindings are pristine. They were freebies from the encyclopedia salesman. Everyone in the family is Buddhist, but nobody is "on fire" for Buddhism the way people in this alcohol and psych unit talk about being "on fire" for Christ. If pressed, my mother and the Math would describe themselves as on fire for atheism. The Math doesn't believe in that which cannot be proven by scientific equation and

documented in triplicate, and my mother couldn't care
less about religion.

I haven't seen Uncle Sen since the day he was
checked into the hospital, and the first few minutes of
my impromptu call, avoiding meeting the Math in my
mother's room, I simply stare at him. He's either used
to having everyone stare at him, or he doesn't notice
my tactless scrutiny. His conversation is all about the
hospital, what it's like for him being here. He is squeaky
clean, shiny and fresh. His skin is completely cleared
up, new as a baby's. Sprawled before me in an easy
host attitude, as though we're sitting in his living room
beneath his collection of Miros and Yamagatas instead
of religious placards and ugly hospital art, he almost
glows, a human lightbulb. When we make eye contact,
the flourescent lights are such that I see my own reflection, yet Uncle Sen somehow seems himself in his own
eyes.

As if reading my thoughts, he muses, "I think the
hardest thing, being here, is starting over." His roommate
leaves for the lounge, and Uncle Sen grimaces. "Well,
hardest thing, that guy bragging about himself, all the
time. Drug addict and drinker," he tells me. "That guy
thinks he's something, all right. Had to be brought in by
a SWAT team, day after me."

I push my hair back, and compose my reply before
opening my mouth. "Learning to live again is a blessing."
For both of you, I want to add, but it's obvious Uncle
Sen isn't far along enough in his program yet to be iden-
tifying with every comrade in detox.

"At twenty, you have a lot of learning opportunities

ahead of you," he says, drawing out "a lot" so it weighs a ton.

My resentment of his condescension makes me struggle to hold my voice level, and respond with, "Some people use up their chances faster than you think."

"Excuse me," he says satirically, "twenty-one."

Easy Does It. I remind myself that he's not going to transform himself from jerk to human overnight. EGO: EASING GOD OUT. LET GO, AND LET GOD. Tearing my attention away from the walls, I say, "I guess you'll miss my birthday party tomorrow."

"I've missed everything," he says, and self-conscious of his own melodrama, he appends, "Worst thing about drunk is, no contact with your own life."

"I know how that is," I say plainly.

"Well, I'm lucky," he says. "All tests came negative. No cirrhosis, no anything else."

"I heard," I tell him.

"Ann called Sally Jasmine," Uncle Sen says.

Uncomfortable, I hesitate. "Really?" I pretend not to have already heard that, too. Sally Jasmine was Uncle Sen's secretary until her husband retired. She quit her job so they could travel together. But her husband died the morning after his retirement party. He was buried with his new gold watch, the back inscribed, "To Robert, For Forty Years of Service." Uncle Sen refused to rehire Sally; he had already employed the first of his fleet of junior college young things.

Aunt Ann called her, and Sally told Aunt Ann she would never have come forth on her own, but while she worked for him, she had told Uncle Sen she would never lie for him, either. Sally told Aunt Ann that with Uncle Sen, it was one woman after another for years.

Aunt Ann has gone to stay with one of her sisters in the city. "I guess you think Ann's done the right thing," Uncle Sen says. "Leaving me."

"Maybe she did what she needed to do for herself."

"Your mother said same thing," Uncle Sen spits. "You're so alike. Ann is hiding from reality. She should be with me."

"I don't imagine you saw much reality through your scotch goggles," I observe. He looks offended, and I relent. "You did seek out more truth than Uncle Mas or Uncle Wes or my mother. But still."

"What?" he barks in frustration. "How would you know?"

"I've been in your office. You kept a record of the truth, anyway."

"Much good it did," Uncle Sen says bitterly.

"It did," I affirm.

"For who? For me?" He snorts. "For you? My daughters? Ashley, too busy to come see me. Jennifer, I dunno, daughter of mine?"

"What do you mean?"

"She came a couple times, didn't say a word to me," Uncle Sen gripes. "Just sat and stared. She looked like a mushroom, looking through her bangs at me. What a dingbat. I dunno how I ever helped her, if I did."

"Yeah." I flip the life preserver around in my hands.

He says, "You can take that, if you want."

"Thanks, no. Well, like you yourself said," I remind him, standing to go, "you have another opportunity now."

"Now," he echoes, and I'm taken by surprise by something I've never seen in Uncle Sen: sincerity and gratitude. I've known him all my life, but suddenly, he looks like a different person than the one I've always known.

"You look great, Uncle Sen." I bend, there's an awkward shuffle of limbs and faces in the right place, and finally I kiss his cheek. He jumps a little, but smiles at me. He smells like honey and fresh water, and when I wipe the splotch of shiny lip color I've left on his cheek, his skin feels like silk.

"Happy birthday, Mina," he says, and motions for me to come close to him. "What's this?" he asks, and pulls a quarter from behind my ear. "Sorry," he says, handing it to me. "All I have."

"Thank you."

"Hey! I've decided not to charge you for the garage repairs," he calls after me.

"Maybe the roof contractor will throw it in at no additional charge."

"You think?"

I leave, take the elevator, and walk slowly to my mother's room. Held overnight for observation, she should be coming home today or tomorrow. Dread weights my footsteps as I enter her room.

She and the Math are murmuring together. The Math told me the doctor had to shave her head, but my mother has a scarf on. She looks up, small and startled, and draws away from the Math. The bed is tiny and narrow, but swaddled in blankets and sunk into her pillows, she looks even smaller. This is a hologram of what my mother appears to be to me: eternally clandestine, conspiring, deceptively wee. But there are lines around her eyes that I've never seen before, and witnessing her immobile in a hospital bed delivers a certain perspective previously unavailable to me. She's on the cusp of late middle age, and she no longer looks beautiful as much as she looks old. Where up until now it wasn't even a question, I can see where it's becoming a sixty-forty split.

Her first words to me are, "You been to see Uncle Sen?"

"I just came from his room. He seems better." I sit on the bed, then move to a chair.

"You can sit on the bed," my mother invites me.

"The three of us? It might break."

"Come sit," she says.

The Math on the right, my mother in the middle, I fix my gaze on a spot on the floor. "How are you feeling?" I ask her at last.

"Okay," she says. "My roommate left this morning, and I haven't gotten another one."

"Uncle Sen is rooming with some sort of outlaw."

"I met him," my mother says, shaking her head, but not for the reason I think. "Everyone in the hospital like this, all our insurance rates go sky high."

"Her diagnosis is good," the Math tells me.

"They say," my mother affirms. "I'll have to go through lots of sensory therapy, but I should be restored in six months."

This entire family is in some sort of therapy. "Restored?"

"When she fell," the Math says, "she damaged part of her brain back here." He indicates the back of her head. "Your mother can't taste or smell."

"You're kidding," I cry, and I think the Math is looking at me funny, but he's just checking his watch.

"It's nothing," my mother dismisses.

"The doctor said she could have gone blind," the Math says. "The brain is amazing."

"Everybody is different," my mother says.

"It all depends on how they develop," the Math says.

"It's nothing," my mother says again.

I recover. "You'll be fine?"

"Fine," she confirms.

"Your flowers," I remind her.

"I can still see," she says. "I'm alive."

"I'm going to cook," the Math says.

"Your father likes to cook," my mother says.

"I'll use spices," he promises.

"Nothing has flavor," she lets me know. "All I get here is Jell-O and hash, but still."

"No," the Math says. "Even nothing has to taste like something."

"Nothing," my mother insists.

The Math checks his watch again. "Do you have change?" he asks me. "I have to put money in the meter."

I dig in my pocket for Uncle Sen's quarter. The Math leaves. My mother yawns like a cat, not covering her mouth. "Tired," she says, shaking her head back and forth.

I ease off the bed. "I'll let you rest."

"Uncle Sen looks good, doesn't he?"

"He really does."

"I couldn't believe it," my mother says. "All of a

sudden, he was a new man. I didn't see him for a day or two, and then I went again, and really looked. All that eczema making him peel, drinking water all the time, no liquor."

"He took me by surprise, too." I sit again. "He made me mad."

"Oh? Why mad?"

"I don't know." I study the floor. "He says that you and I are alike, and by insinuation, that he's different."

She looks thoughtful. "You agree?"

"I don't know either of you well enough to say."

"I'm your mother," she says, a little of her snap returning, "he's your uncle. What don't you know?"

"It's not so simple."

"You don't need to know us any other way."

I smooth my hair, and try to think. "I guess," I muse, "seeing him, and listening to him, I couldn't understand what Uncle Sen has done to be rewarded with a new skin."

I expected her to tell me it's not my place to understand, but instead she nods her head. "I couldn't understand it, either," she marvels almost enthusiastically. "I think, on one hand, it's not our place to understand. But it bothered me so much, I couldn't help but think and think. This bed, so uncomfortable, I stayed up all night, thinking. I look at Uncle Sen, and I wondered why suddenly, he gets to know peace. Why him? Grandma never had any peace. Ojiichan never had any peace. Uncle Masa, Uncle Wes, me, we've been lucky. But Uncle Sen has always been luckiest of all, even now."

"So, um, have you spoken to Uncle Mas, since—" I hesitate, "—yesterday?"

"No, but Emiko-san brought those," she says, indicating an explosion of iris. "Store bought."

I inspect the arrangement. "Pretty vase."

" 'The void in the vase is what makes it empty,' " my mother quotes. "Lao-Tzu. I think I read that on Uncle Sen's wall."

"No, no," I laugh, "it's, 'The void in the vase is what makes it valuable.' "

She looks so surprised. "Really?"

"I'm almost certain." It's bad manners, but I'm laughing so hard, I have to leave the room.

Void, vase, empty: my mother. Like so many, she believes that the greatest measurement of life is in gain, when in reality, the greatest measurement of life is in loss. After a while, standing alone, I wipe away the tears with the backs of my hands.

Wet Dreams

~~~~~~~~~

I'm wearing white and watching the sky, purple clouds rolling past like plums in God's own fruit derby. It hurts my neck, but I crane it upward anyway. The muscles are tight and the angle of my head constricts my throat, and yet, I still do all I can to breathe. When I wake up, safe in my bed, I'm gasping for air.

The doctor says I seem balanced. I imagine my head flat as a table, medication bottles on top of it all sliding off to the right. I check my watch, and tell the doctor I ran into my cousin Hope here last week, and today saw Yolanda Gotanda, granddaughter of the hardware store family, at the information desk. I tell him about the ancient turtle emerging from his warm orange and gold sea in my childhood. In the past few weeks, I've noticed he doesn't come around here anymore. The doctor says that a loggerhead turtle symbolizes the penis.

I burst out laughing. I can't help myself. It's just too Freudian. I slap my sides. I mean, as it turns out, all those dreams, all those years when I was a girl, I was dreaming about the very thing I wanted to become.

In the ranch orchard, there is, in the far northeast corner of the property, a wild almond tree. By far the largest tree in the grove, it dominates the orchard. It grew there of its own accord. It was used as a shade tree and lunch spot by field workers until the orchard was fenced in. Trimming it one year, a branch fell on Ojiichan's arm, breaking the face of his watch. It flowers every spring, scattering pollen and petals to the four winds. University agriculturalists come twice a year to check the orchard and remedy the tree's boron deficiency. It produces more nuts than any other tree yields fruit, and no matter how many buckets of nuts my mother takes to friends, the supply seems perpetually undiminished.

A road runs by it, and crows fly over it, but the ground beneath the laden branches is covered with golden almonds still in their shells. The almonds are sweeter than any others, sweeter than any fruit. Runaway chickens from miles around roost in its shade, but the almonds are untouched, their shells too hard for the crows to crack. The Swan Girls and I used to pretend they were valuable stones or minerals, like diamonds on South African beaches just waiting for a lucky prospector to come along. I gather a bunch of them together to snack on, and remember what

it felt like to think we were discovering gold right outside
our front door.

Inside the house, the Math sits in an updated version
of Ojiichan's old reclining chair and watches Oprah inter-
rogate this horrible couple who aren't together anymore
and in fact want to kill each other. The woman even shows
the audience the check she made out to a man she reached
through *Soldier of Fortune* magazine. However, it turns out
that she didn't send the check at the last minute, and now
the couple plans to marry.

"Each other?" I ask incredulously, trekking through
the living room to find the nutcracker in the extra utensil
pantry off the den. "True love," I marvel, digging out
the nutcracker.

The phone rings. "If it's one of your aunts, give
them the directions to the restaurant," the Math says,
glancing at me. "By the phone."

Because the cook is out of commission, tonight's food
is coming from a Chinese restaurant. Today is the day the
Math was supposed to motor to Osno, but he and my
aunts are organizing my birthday party instead. I told them
not to worry about it, but my mother insisted, and from
her hospital phone, arranged to have the party catered.
The Math is picking her up from the hospital today, my
aunts are getting and bringing the food, and one of the
Swan Girls is in charge of the cake.

"I'm ready," my mother says.

"She's ready," I relay to the Math.

The phone rings again a couple seconds later, and as
he struggles into his shoes, the Math repeats the line about
my aunts.

"Wil?"

It's the ex. My cue comes and goes. "Are you in jail or something?" I ask finally, the only reason I can think of that he would call.

"Who told you that?"

Levity rarely works to my benefit. "Some protest, right?"

"The tuition hike."

"That's worthwhile," I allow, still glad that I wasn't the one taken by paddywagon to the police station to wait until someone made bail for me. I've had opportunities to be arrested at PCU while the ex and I were together, but what it always boiled down to was the fact that I just wasn't interested.

"Did you see my picture in the paper? The *Free Press?*" he asks.

The PCU rag. "Sorry. Did you look like a hardcore radical?"

"Yeah. I liked it. Well," he shifts gears, "I just called to wish you a happy birthday. You're legal!"

"Heck, I'm unsafe at any speed." I pop an almond into my mouth. "I thought I'd gotten my present from you early."

"What would that be?"

"I ran into your friend recently, you know, square versus well-rounded meals? He's like, 'Congrats getting sprung from the insane asylum, Wil.' Thanks a lot."

Here we go. "He didn't say it like that."

"The point is, he said something. When I called you from the bin, I asked you not to say anything to anyone, and you agreed."

He's arrived at nasty, with a vengeance and a whine.

"When you called, you yelled at me, you blamed me for putting you there! You blaaamed me," he bleats. "Everyone was at my place, when I got off the phone I was totally freaked out, I haaad to tell them."

"Square versus well-rounded wasn't."

"Wasn't what?"

"Wasn't at your place. He was in Alaska, waist-deep in fish, trying to meet the barmaid or ecologist of his dreams." Then the plural pronoun hits me, as though it should even be a bombshell. "What do you mean, 'everyone?' "

"You bitch," the ex snarls. "You always did twist around everything I said."

We've had better birthdays together, exchanging poems and kisses and being silly. The last thing I gave the ex was a tie, about as suitable for him as a set of Samsonite for a duck going south for the winter. I never saw the ex wear it, which is just as well. I guess it was my way of tying the ex into something he would never be.

I pull the phone away from my head to look at it, like that's somehow going to help me see. I thought that as time passed the ex would improve, but he seems to only get worse. When we speak now, we're just like all those blockheads populating the daytime TV talkshows, the ones who accuse the sitter, the grandma, and each other of setting up a crack lab in the bathroom, molesting the kids, deifying the devil. Listening to his distorted squawks coming out of the receiver, I think who is this awful man?

I can't think of anything to say, so I remain silent. On one hand, I hope the ex figures things out and gets some of the peace he's never had but knows he wants so badly. I hate to witness him going *boom-boom-boom* down the karmic ladder. Yet another part of me, the part that can't help but be on the verge of a nonexistent second trimester, would savor seeing him lose the rest of his hair.

Hair, relationships, dreams: Loss is livable, but maybe it's the grief and memory of what's gone that people can't live with. Maybe the ex can't survive this loss if it's in his face reminding him all the time. Or maybe he just never wants to see me again because he hates me. But I can take it all as the ultimate reverse compliment: People only rage at and about people and things that they once loved, or still do.

"You know," the ex mewls, "I'm not some cold, unfeeling bastard. It hurts a lot to hear you say some of the things you say."

I gawk. "You mean after all of this, I'm supposed to have sympathy for you, too?" This is the worst part of all, because I do, and now I can tell the difference between understanding and charity.

I hate what we've become, but I don't hate him. I still want to tell the ex about the abortion, because he's the only person with whom it should be rightfully shared. Yet, when he squeals, "Don't you dare pity me," I realize that to tell him at this point would be the same as dumping a plant out of its pot, exposing its roots: Exposing myself to the ex wouldn't kill me, but telling him now wouldn't release me from my burden, either; it would be giving away something of myself for free.

I go on with saying that in ways neither of us ever

intended, I learned a lot from him. Despite our melodramatic finale, I want to hold on to that.

"I'm sorry, but you have to let me go," he says.

"I think I can hold on to everything I learned without holding on to you."

"You blaaamed me," he jeers, sounding almost satisfied, seemingly content in the free-floating anger he in fact despairs over and struggles to divest himself of.

"Gee, talking to you," I tell him, "I realize that I'm just the diagnosed person, here."

The same as the last time we spoke at the grocery, there's a silence, and the ex says, "Good luck, Wil." It's obvious he thinks I need it. The people who most need to stop rationalizing the truth are usually the least likely to do so, in diametrical opposition to luck: The people most lacking in luck are the likeliest to believe in its existence.

We hang up. Maybe being lucky to lose love at a young age really means that the bereft has time to recover, and recover right. Losing love hurts like hell, but next time, I think I'll know how to care for myself, and for that love.

"I forgive you," I say aloud, and this time I do laugh, partly because I'm talking to myself and feel nutty in a way that I know isn't nutty at all, but mostly because I'm not forgiving the ex so much as I've got the permission I need to forgive myself, for practically everything.

I couldn't take Ojiichan's hand when he reached out from his recliner. I never knew what to do with the ex's heart when I had it. My mother isn't what I want her to be any more than I'm what she wants me to be. I don't know and can't know my uncles, and never will. It's no one's fault, nobody's to blame. I've been too young and impatient to understand before now, caught up in my juvenile fantasies and illusions of what people should be, rather than what they are, the possibilities triumphing over the actualities in my imagination.

At twenty-one, I'm finally hanging my defective adolescent dreams out to dry. They flap and wave at me as they call back their tender, exonerating goodbyes.

Swan Girl

~~~~~~~~

Half of my grandparents' ashes are stored at their prefectural church back in Japan. The other half are in a predominately Japanese-American mausoleum ten minutes away from the ranch. It's convenient, not only because it's nearby, but because we can visit the whole family at once, Ojiichan and my grandmother, Uncle Mas and Aunt Em's stillborn son, and the baby aunts who died in the camp. (The latter were exhumed after the war, and were brought to California.)

Everybody bought their niches at the same time. My parents have the niche below my grandparents. My uncles have one each on either side of my grandparents. Nobody in the family bought niches above my grandparents. It would be disrespectful to occupy a higher place. A long time ago, my mother told me if I want to, I can be in the niche with the Math and her. It holds four urns comfortably, though two would have to be in back. "You could arrange to have us rotated periodically," I suggested, "a revolving star billing thing." With the proviso that she and the Math approve of my future husband, my mother said that the unknown man is welcome to join us. In her mind, she was offering me a great treat instead of every teen's worst nightmare, an eternal double date with her parents.

To the immediate left of where my parents will be are the baby aunts. Everyone jokingly calls the dead sisters the doctor and the lawyer of the family because it was my grandparents' dream to have a doctor and a lawyer among their children.

But if they couldn't become either one, then their children could marry them. On the day of my birthday, at the front door at the ranch, are Joy and her husband, Kent the nosebobber, whose polyester pomposity combined with the pretentious combustion that erupts from his mouth every time he open it makes listeners long for an extinguisher. His personal and professional motto appears to be, "The best offense is a good defense." Maybe it's a straightforward little-man-wants-to-rule-the-world Napoleon complex, but dealing with him makes me feel like saying, "Gee, sorry about your penis."

My cousin Joy has been programmed from birth to entertain nothing but synthetic thoughts. She shimmies into the entryway, hands off the baby to Faith so she can greet my mother, who thinks Joy is a doll. Joy makes a huge deal over my mother's bandaged head, all pats and

coos and compliments. My mother tells Joy she can neither
smell nor taste for an estimated six months. Once revived,
Joy dries her tears and drops her voice to a whisper, pre-
sumably dissecting Uncle Sen, whom she just heard about
today.

In a more conventional social vein, Joy flatters my
mother on her blouse and lipstick. My mother replies it's
a terrible shade on her; she shouldn't have let the salesgirl
talk her into such a young red. She leans toward Faith to
simper at Joy's baby, who lets out a glass-shattering howl.
"Oh, oh," my mother frets, and kitchy-koos him, which
makes him cry louder. Meanwhile, wailing for attention
in a silent scream, Kent and Joy's other small hostage to
fortune, Junior, lashes Joy's legs with his clip-on tie, already smeared with seafood spread from the appetizer
tray.

Grace arrives, bearing a gift. It's a pink electric blanket for my birthday, apologizing for not having time to
wrap it. Humans used to huddle together in caves for
warmth and comfort. Now we buy our cancer blankets,
and create communities of one. Grace tells me that she
didn't have time to wrap the blanket because she's involved with an architect.

"But do I hear wedding bells?" Joy asks on her way
into the kitchen to get a washcloth for her stockings. She
twinkles at Grace as she passes. Then she turns on me.
"For either of you?"

"I'm twenty," I scowl. "Twenty-one," I remember.

But she's already past me, in the kitchen greeting her
mother with a kiss Aunt Em shrivels from. Aunt Em dis-
likes physical contact. Grace turns my way again. "He's

rich, too,'' she says, meaning the architect. She stares over at her father, Uncle Sen, who looks like a fugitive at the snack tray with Uncle Wes, back from his vacation.

"He's probably gay," I tell Grace, meaning her architect.

"I don't know," she says apprehensively. "Do you think?"

I shrug, and kick my feet. Grace says, "I don't know" a lot, and she's not kidding. Her passivity annoys me. I look around to share an eyeroll with someone. Uncle Mas drifts away, oblivious to my exchange with his daughter. It's oft repeated wisdom that if Grace, who's a thriving computer engineer with a condo of her own and lots of friends from work and church, could only find a man, she would be a better woman.

"Only kidding," I say, feeling bad suddenly. "Thanks for the blanket."

Going through the kitchen to take the blanket to my room, my mother and Aunt Em are comparing head injuries. Aunt Em was once involved in a three-car pile-up wherein her head was whipsawed into the windshield. Overhead, balloons that Kent and Joy brought bob up and down. The balloons are driving Aunt Em's corgis crazy. The Math directs Junior to take the dogs outside, then helps him. Faith jangles her bracelets and asks if the carrots for the dip tray should be cut in circles or lengths for maximum nutritional benefits. She's been ignoring me since she presented me with a makeover certificate and I told her if she set me up on another blind date, I'd kill her.

"Jeff is nice," Faith protested.

"I have to be alone for a while," I told her.

"Why?" She looked at me like I was crazy. "I'm never alone."

"Yeah, and that's just part of your problem."

Aunt May, bearing stuffed pasta shells, is relegated to a sideline role, admiring my mother's table linens. Joy opens cupboard after cupboard, looking for a glass. The Math comes in, wipes the dog drool off his shoes, and tries to involve Jennifer in a discussion about social work, her field of employ. Jennifer has brought Aunt Ann and a dozen lillies. Kent labors to chat up Uncle Mas, who grunts his responses and avoids all eye contact.

They barely speak the same language, and they're unable to hear one another anyway. Past their rivalries and the seamless assimilation with white America that Ojiichan stressed to all of us, there's an emotional and psychological void around them all like a life-sucking black hole. Through my closed bedroom door, I can hear them nattering madly about their latest professional accomplishments, recent purchases, little victories, and defeats they turn into funny stories, always conscientious to evoke laughter instead of pity.

Today, after the Math brought my mother home, she asked me to cut some gerbera daisies and to accompany her to the mausoleum. Driving a car is a rare pleasure for me, even with my mother in it: "Turn right. Not so fast. Get in the other lane. Hurry up."

In the courtyard of the mausoleum, stone *ohakas* of Japanese-American families are lined up in rows. In Japanese, the *ha* in *ohaka* is the same as the *ba* in *obake*, meaning "apparition." No spirits were making themselves apparent to me; all that was immediately evident was the cool inner sanctum of the courtyard, the mute stones before me, and an occasional ringing phone from mausoleum offices seemingly far away.

I took the old flowers to the sink, discarded them, and filled the holders with water. My mother asked how the gerberas smelled and I felt awful. I told her they didn't smell so great and stuffed them willy-nilly into the holders, where they twirled around on the rims. We both prayed for a moment, trading the one ring of prayer beads back and forth, then I turned to go.

"*Kanji*, English," my mother said, lingering, reading both inscriptions on each urn. "Two cultures woven together. You and Grandma were the same, but opposite: She was more Japanese than American."

I returned to read over her shoulder.

"It's the difference between shame and guilt," my mother observed. "Those flowers look lopsided."

"How do you mean?"

"Shame is Japanese," my mother said immediately. "Trim the stem on that one, Mina. Japanese shame each other into conformity. Needs of the individual are not so important as society and family. It means, we worry more about what people will think of us than what we actually do."

"Guilt is American?" I asked, slipping the short flower stem into my pocket.

"Americans have fixed moral standards, are taught to have personal consciences that make them feel guilty when they do bad things. To a Japanese, mercy can be okay when the family or society is at risk."

"But what if the babies could have lived?"

It just slipped out of my mouth like a natural fact.

For a moment, I grappled with the urge to blurt out an apology, but my mother spoke first.

"Mama was dealt the worst possible combination: She acted as a Japanese person, but felt like an American. Sometimes, you do what you think will be best for all involved, but afterward, you know your best wasn't your best. On your American side, you know you didn't uphold the moral aspect." My mother touched the *ohaka*, wherein the spirits rest, and put her prayer beads back into her purse.

"What if the babies had been boys?" I asked as we leave. "Would their lives have been more valuable?"

She blinked. "I don't know." Then, "Probably."

I held the door for her. "Is that Japanese," I asked, "or American?"

"No," she said. "Life."

"Life is plain old hard," I stated, looking to her.

"It's not fair, either," she admitted. "If anything, Mama's ideals were too high."

"How do you mean?"

"She expected certain things, that's the way she was raised. But nothing is free," she told me, approaching the car. "When your ideals are high, you have to pay for them."

In Japanese, "high ideals" are *riso takai*. *Riso* are ideals. *Takai* means both "high" and "expensive." Ideals are expensive. Driving the same road as the other day, returning from shopping and Ann Sayles's, almond shells crackled and popped beneath the tires, crows swooped above us. My mother leaned forward, one hand on the dashboard, to look directly into the sky.

"Crows and cars," she whispered, and we both giggled.

I switched radio stations, and my mother turned the music up, tapping her hands without consideration of the beat. I thought about shame and guilt, Japanese and American, duty and sin. Sin is "One Size Fits All." Big sins, small sins, everywhere a sin, sin. It's like all the possible combinations of "undutiful." I added them up like imaginary cribbage hands in my mind.

Aunt Ann and Jennifer leave beforehand, but my mother insists on fixing plates of food for them. Dinner consists of ten Chinese dishes, Aunt May's pasta shells, and sashimi Uncle Mas caught and had frozen at home.

As they loosen belts, sip tea, and clean their teeth, I tell the family, "In Japan, they celebrate the sixtieth birthday because that's when you've completed the Japanese zodiac cycle, so you've reached your second childhood. But this time, you're at the height of your wisdom."

"We aren't in Japan," Joy says. "Pass the sweet and sour, Stretch."

While the women clear the table and the Math shows Kent something he recently received from his broker, I slip out to the veranda following Uncle Mas, who's enjoying a cigarette away from the scrutiny of his wife and children. Tonight they had first dressed him down bilingually, then batted the cigarettes from his lips as he tried to light them. When Aunt Em went to the bathroom, he skulked outside and lit up.

Uncle Mas used to take care of Ojiichan when my mother had somewhere to go and the Math was at work. The other uncles stayed away. My mother would return home to find Ojiichan watching TV, Uncle Mas asleep on the floor under a blanket Ojiichan had thrown over him.

"Come inside," my mother calls to us from the window above the sink. She's running water over the dinner dishes. "Joy's getting the cake ready."

I acknowledge her, and turn back to Uncle Mas. Those whom I like, I want to think feel mutually toward me. Uncle Mas's muddy little eyes in his nut brown face are unreadable in the dark. Gemini, the twins, is alight up above, and Orion shines. The kitchen behind us is both dark and bright with the blaze of birthday candles being lit one by one, the Swan Girls twittering together over the cake, plates, and ice cream.

It's so clear out tonight. No rain tomorrow, which means good planting weather. The veranda has always been the most aromatic spot in the house, the place where everyone used to gather on summer nights after dinner, where we would sit and talk about days long past, The Wish Bait, sometimes about camp and Ojiichan's village in Japan, where ancient turtles rose and went to shore. From here, I can almost smell the sea intermingled with clean lemony soap and warm oven air, even if the oven was only used to warm the take-out food. Blooms and blossoms mingle in a tangle of hot, tender perfumes that waft up from the garden below.

My mother tends her garden well. From her, I learned how to care for plants and flowers, cinnamon carnations and candystripe, Johnny-jump-ups and white roses. My mother was an easy horticulturalist, telling me the names of the flowers as "dark-eyed gerbera ladies" instead of plain old gerbera daisies, stuffing the hose down the back of my little tank shirt, stopping for a moment from her weeding to hold a felled buttercup beneath my chin, seeing if I liked butter. Her touch was gentle and grave as she checked the dim yellow reflection against my skin.

"Sometimes it seems as though we've spent our entire lives on this veranda," I muse, smoothing my hair. "From here, you see everything." When he says nothing, I gesture out and upward. "Look, Orion lights up the sky tonight."

"Don't see. Come on," Uncle Mas says, casting the butt away, and getting up.

The lights are dimmed, and the cake is an inferno of twenty-one candles. A scattering of my mother's violets' shy faces glow between "leaves" of halved almonds. It must be around this age that people stop having birthday cakes with candles on them, except on the occasion of practical jokes disguised as surprise parties by cruel friends.

I notice that three pieces of the cake are missing, sent to the hospital with Aunt Ann and Jennifer. "Enough to go around?" My mother worries, looking around the table.

The family doesn't sing "Happy Birthday," they never do. "I wanna flower piece," Junior says, mesmerized by the radiant cake.

"Hurry up," my mother says. "It's melting fast."

Aunt May drops the spoons she's handing out. My mother glances her way at the clatter, and masks her distaste with an imperceptible shake of her head. A lifetime of training reflects in her every gesture. She never got over Aunt May's fatal potluck faux pas years ago, when Aunt May brought a Chinese chicken salad with dark meat in it.

"Blow them out!" Junior screams.

"Go on, Wil," my mother says. It's on the tip of my tongue to encourage her the same way she encourages me: Go on, Mom. But she would never get it in a million years, and it's not my duty to show her.

I look at them, and they look at me. I close my eyes. Past a certain point, it's impossible to manufacture ignorant bliss. But if things work out the way they should, people who want it badly enough are eventually delivered the real thing.

I'm turning twenty-one today. By the Japanese method, I'm a little less than forty years away from my own happily ever after.

"Make a wish," my mother sings, and claps her hands.

I breathe deep.

Acknowledgments

I owe a great debt to Suzanne Wickham-Beaird, whose friendship and wise counsel are my privilege. I thank Liza Landsman and Merrilee Heifetz at Writers' House for their efforts on my behalf. Peter Borland is a great editor. Lisa Healy helped me find my voice. My belated, heartfelt thanks to Susan Magrino.

I am both grateful and beholden to Pamela and Paul Mari Petrowsky for so generously sharing with me their wisdom and experience. Their elegant, eloquent insights turn dead horses into glue factories every time.

Cal Lin has shown me many brotherly kindnesses on both coasts.

Henry and Kay Yamada are friends as well as uncles. Their confidence in me is my honor to uphold.

The Radetskys were kind to me. Meeting Steven Cooper was the best part of college. Peri Good: Thank you.

Virginia Alonso, Frances Bruton, Lopez, Chin, and Lopez, Gail Reese, and Laura Ward have been mainstays of support and laughs in New Mexico.

The Dalys, Peter Dees, and Diann Edmunds are friends from midwestern days long ago.

My father is a citadel of response, reliability, and love. My mother helped me become myself.

There are many others from whom I have learned lots, but two stand out as extra-special. Eta Lin, thanks for being my best friend, and William Jay: Thank you for making me want to sing.